THE LOST CONCERTO

Book Two of the
Alexis Brooks Series

SANDRA MILLER

The
Lost Concerto

The Lost Concerto
Published by Onda Mountain Books

Cover Art
Musical vignette LXVIII © Odyssei | Dreamstime.com
Crosshair sight © Blojfo | Dreamstime.com
Thoughtful violinist © Hongqi Zhang (aka Michael Zhang)
| Dreamstime.com

Cover Design and Text @2013 by Sandra Miller

Discover other titles by Sandra Miller at
www.sandra-miller.com

RITORNELLO:
The Nightmare

The dream started with a scream.

"He's got that poor girl! Somebody stop him!"

I reached into my purse and hauled out a silenced pistol, running out into the street, taking as careful aim as I could manage under the circumstances.

Snick, snick--two silenced shots in quick successions.

"It's just another day at the firing range," I muttered to myself.

--snick, snick--

"--just another few targets down at the range--"

--snick, snick--

"--just a group of targets that happen to be spinning, and moving away from you, and in uncomfortably close proximity to people." I lowered the pistol and wiped the sweat from my forehead.

Six shots fired, four tires blown out, no casualties. The car screeched and swerved to an undignified halt, sideways in the street like a toy car tossed aside by a giant child.

The back door flew open and a man came charging out, brandishing a weapon and cursing so quickly it was impossible to pick out individual words.

"You just cannot stop interfering, can you, woman? You could have left well enough alone and lived, but no--you keep making yourself a thorn in my side! No more, do you hear me? No more!"

He raised that big gun.

I was numb with fear, I couldn't feel my hands or my feet--but I understood what I had to do. I pulled the pistol up and lined the sights up with that hateful, horrible man, squeezed the trigger--

--and heard the hollow click of an empty cartridge. I was out, and I was dead.

MOVEMENT ONE:
History Repeats

The first time I saw the Zwickauer Mulde, I wondered how it would feel to throw myself into a river like that one.

I suppose I should have accepted that as an omen, and demanded that we fly back to America that instant.

Instead I shrugged it off and turned away from the passenger-side window of the rented Mercedes. Jet lag could do strange things to a person. The midnight drive to the Dayton airport...the layover in Chicago...the seemingly endless flight to Leipzig...Alexis and I hadn't slept properly for far too long.

He glanced at me, then back at the road. "Are you okay over there?"

I smiled, but it felt kind of weak. "Didn't Robert Schumann throw himself into this river?"

"No. That was the Rhine. He was born in Zwickau,

remember?"

I nodded. I really *was* jet-lagged if I had forgotten that. Schumann's birth in 1810 in this town was the whole reason we were here, after all. One week from today--June eighth, Schumann's birthday, and coincidentally our first wedding anniversary--the Philharmoniker Zwickauer would have a special concert. In celebration of the one-hundredth anniversary of the great composer's birth, they contracted Alexis to perform Schumann's Violin Concerto in D minor with them. The concert had been sold out for weeks.

I was along for the ride, but I didn't seem to be enjoying it very much. This was my very first trip outside the United States, and I had been impossible to live with for months, crazy with excitement.

And yet, since we had arrived in Germany, a pall had fallen over my mood. I was gripped by a peculiar melancholy, filled with an unspeakable dread. I wasn't afraid that something bad was going to happen.

I was certain of it.

"You aren't still thinking about that crazy phone call, are you?" Alexis's tone was deliberately, falsely light.

I glanced at him, then quickly turned back to the window. "No. No, of course not."

Of course I was, and he was, too, whether either of us would admit it or not.

"It didn't mean anything, you know," he said conversationally.

"I know."

"It was just a prank, or she was a couple sandwiches

short of a picnic."

"I know," I repeated.

She hadn't sounded like a joker, though, and she hadn't sounded crazy. She had sounded perfectly sincere, and she had begged us not to go to Germany. Alexis had answered the call, and what he'd heard upset him enough that he signaled me to pick up the extension.

"You could have your choice of venue, Mr. Brooks, any where in the world. Please, do not go to Germany. Not now. I beg this of you. Nothing good will come of this trip."

The voice was utterly unfamiliar. The woman had given no name. Caller information had been blocked.

There was not a single rational reason to take her seriously, or to give any thought to anything she said. At least, that was what I kept telling myself, pushing aside the memory of that dream. I mean, it was just a crazy dream. Right?

And yet, I couldn't seem to get that phone call out of my head.

Nothing good will come of this trip.

Maybe I could have better ignored it if I hadn't secretly agreed.

It was late in the afternoon when Alexis pulled the Mercedes to a smooth stop in front of the Hotel Sachsen Zwickau. It sprawled across the rich green countryside, more of a resort than a hotel, with a beautiful view of the river, and flowering bushes exploding into bright colors all around the neatly whitewashed buildings.

I stepped out of the car and stretched. It was almost

painful after so many hours in confined spaces. "This is not in town," I remarked. "You're going to have a bit of a drive to rehearsals."

Alexis walked around the front of the car to join me. "Yes, but isn't it worth it?"

I couldn't deny it. I looked around again at the crisp colors and gorgeous views, overwhelmed by the fresh, heady scent of blooming flowers.

Alexis grinned at me. "Come on, Mrs. Brooks, let's go get checked in." He took my arm and we went into the lobby.

"Let's go get checked out, is more like it," I muttered under my breath, feeling the heat of a blush rise high in my cheeks. As soon as we walked into the room, people stopped what they were doing and stared at Alexis. Other people turned to see what the first people were looking at, and then they stared, too. Pretty soon the entire room stood stock-still, staring at my husband as though they had never seen a concert violinist before.

Did I mention that Alexis Brooks is also an international superstar?

A smattering of applause ran around the room, then dissipated. Alexis ducked his head and went to the check-in counter.

For some reason that little display rubbed me the wrong way. I mean, I adored Alexis as much as anyone--obviously-- but he hadn't even done anything yet. I suppose I had become spoiled by my time in Newton, become accustomed to being his only fan, having him all to myself.

Or maybe it was just the J-word again. Honestly, I was dead on my feet. There was just no way I was thinking rationally. Of course people appreciated Alexis. That was what I wanted, wasn't it? Wasn't that part of the reason I had worked so hard to clear his name?

The girl behind the counter had gleaming red hair worked into thick braids that wrapped around her head. She smiled at Alexis like she had completely forgotten where she was, and maybe even who she was. "Willkommen," she said. "Welcome to the Hotel Sachsen Zwickau."

"Thank you. My wife and I have a reservation."

"Of course." She typed rapidly on the computer in front of her, then pulled a couple of plastic card keys from a drawer at her side. She swiped each of them through a magnetic strip scanner on the side of the keyboard, then tucked them into an envelope and handed it to Alexis. "I do hope you will enjoy your stay," she said sweetly, and smiled that dreamy smile again.

Irritation flashed through me again. I smothered it quickly, ashamed of myself. How had I lost it so completely, so fast? Jealous, because a hotel clerk smiled at my husband? I must have been more tired and grouchy than I had realized.

At least, I hoped that was all it was.

If you are anything like me, you tend to stay in the same sort of places when you travel. Two-star, national chains, decent rates, plain rooms, basically the same everywhere you go.

This background did very little to prepare me for our stay at the Hotel Sachsen Zwickau.

"This isn't a room," I said, staring.

Alexis laughed. I didn't know if everything struck him as funny today, or if he was just trying to raise my spirits. "No. This way I can practice without disturbing you."

I stood in a sitting room, complete with sofa and armchair. It opened on either side to bedrooms, each with its own small bathroom. One room had a king-sized bed, the other a double, but they were both topped with fluffy featherbeds.

And every available surface held bright bouquets of flowers. The rooms were filled with the scent of them--I had a feeling this was a gesture not extended to every guest.

My suspicion was confirmed when I looked through the archway on the left--the big bed held boxes of chocolates, bottles of wine, and cards from what must have been every staff member at the hotel.

"It seems," I said dryly, "you have some fans here."

Alexis looked over my shoulder and laughed out loud. "Now that hasn't happened in a while." He put his hands on my shoulders, suddenly serious. "And I hope you realize that it's all thanks to you. If it hadn't been for you, the welcome, the flowers, even this concert--none of it would have happened."

I nodded, but I couldn't help sneaking another glance at the display on the bed, tangible evidence of other people's renewed affection for him. How long would he need me, now that he had the world at his feet again?

After we saw our luggage safely into the suite, we took Alexis's violin and mine into the bathroom, propped the cases open, and turned the shower on to hot water. Our humidifiers had run dry during the interminable ride in the bone-dry air of jet planes, but we figured a few hours in a humid bathroom should have the violins feeling normal again.

I stomped back out into the bedroom, shoved the mess on the bed over to one side, and flopped unceremoniously down in the clear spot I had created. I couldn't explain my sour mood, but as the day dragged on, it was getting harder and harder not to give in to it.

Alexis sat down on the edge of the bed, next to me. "What's wrong? I know you're tired, but it isn't like you to be this out of sorts."

I sighed and rubbed a hand across my face. "You're right. I'm sorry. I just--I can't shake the feeling that something bad is going to happen."

"Hmm." Alexis made a show of taking my pulse and checking my forehead. "Well--considering it's your first day in a foreign country, after fifteen hours on planes and in cars--do you know what I think?"

"I'm jet-lagged?" My tone was as black as my mood.

"No. Well, maybe. But more than that, you are hungry. Come with me and let's get some dinner. You'll feel like a whole different person."

"I don't know," I said doubtfully. "I'm not sure it's a good idea to go anywhere. I'm telling you, something wicked this way comes."

"That's just the jet lag talking." He took my hands and pulled me up from the bed. "Come, eat. You know you want to."

I gave up. I never could really tell Alexis no. He was right,

I was hungry.

And I had to admit, a whole new person sounded pretty good right then.

♫

The restaurant at the Hotel Sachsen Zwickau was good; you could tell that as soon as you walked in. It was also probably targeted at tourists, with its German flags, beer steins, and nutcrackers on display. There were lots of windows--the same kind we had in our rooms--large and square, with wooden frames that opened inwards on hinges. They were set back into arches in the walls.

Alexis spoke quietly to the hostess, and she led us quickly and without fuss to a room in the back with a single large table in it, and cuckoo clocks on every available bit of wall space. From very small to really big, some with photographs of mountains, some with weather-forecasting figurines-- there were more types of clocks than I had ever imagined, all with chains and weights, all ticking together at slightly different intervals. It seemed like it would have been annoying, but I actually found it relaxing. It was Geppetto's workshop, and I got to eat there.

Unfortunately I didn't know anything about German food, not even enough to guess what might be good on the menu. I gave up and asked Alexis to order me whatever he was having.

We ended up with fresh, warm, brown bread, oven-fried potatoes with lots of paprika, and veal cutlets with a heavy mushroom sauce.

It was delicious. And as Alexis had promised, I felt like a whole new person. We sat talking over Black Forest cake and coffee until all of those cuckoo clocks started clamoring at once--for the second time since we had been in there.

"That," Alexis said, "was probably our cue to go get some sleep."

I nodded, regarding ruefully the cake left on my plate. German food was heavy and the portions had been huge, and we could have sat there another three hours and I still wouldn't have been able to finish it. It had been wonderful, though.

I walked back to the room hand in hand with Alexis, under the clear skies and sparkling stars of a new country, the most relaxed I had been in days.

Rampant destruction met us inside the sitting room. Furniture had been overturned and slashed, end tables splintered and broken. The hundreds of flowers had been torn and trampled, their vases shattered. Our luggage had been viciously cut through, our clothes and belongings ripped and shredded and thrown about the room.

I ran into the big bedroom and turned on the light. There were feathers scattered all over the room. The sheets hung from the bed in ragged tatters; the mattress had been slashed down to the springs. Drawers hung brokenly out of the dresser frame, and the room stank of the wine puddled in the carpet from the shattered bottles on the floor.

"The other room is the same," Alexis said from behind me, and then I heard his sharp intake of breath. "Except for that."

On the wall above the headboard was a messy, finger-painted message. It could have been anything, but it looked like blood.

GO HOME

♪

"I don't understand." My hands were clasped tightly in front of me, but the tremor in my voice gave me away. "Why would someone do all of this and leave our violins? Not that I'm complaining, but it doesn't make sense."

The hotel security manager shook his head. Wilhelm Braun was a short, compact man who exuded competence. "That part is easy." His English was heavily accented, but fluent. "The shower was running. The intruder assumed it was in use. He evidently had no wish to attack you personally. This--" he waved a hand at the general devastation of the room around us, "--it was a warning."

"But from who? Who would do this?" Alexis put his arm around my shoulders as he spoke. My fingers crept up to his, seeking reassurance. I always felt better when he was with me, even now. Especially now.

"I wish I knew. I wish I could tell you for certain. But Maestro--I should let you know that not everyone here is a fan."

"No, of course not, but--"

"I speak not for myself, Maestro," he continued hastily. "I assure you I have the utmost confidence in you and the police of your country. But there are those, I am afraid, who still regard you as a monster."

"A monster." Alexis surveyed the destruction around us,

and his jaw worked silently.

"We had a call," I said hesitantly, "before we left the States. A woman told us we shouldn't come here. She said nothing good would come of it."

He spread his hands, as if that proved his point. "Just so. Some people, they feel the need to take things into their own hands. If you will come with me, Maestro, Frau, we will need to take a statement from you for our police report. Then we will get you into new rooms."

We were only too happy to turn our backs on the wrecked suite and follow Mr. Braun outside.

"I *told* you something bad was going to happen," I grumbled under my breath.

Alexis squeezed my shoulders. "Lucky guess."

I didn't say anything. It sure didn't feel very lucky to me.

At the end of our very long night, the hotel offered to put us into another suite identical to the one we lost. I declined in a kind of horror, and asked if we could have a regular room instead. Right then the thought of Alexis practicing in one room while I sat alone in another didn't appeal to me at all.

So in the end we took our violins and the bags full of toiletries the hotel manager had given us and settled into a regular hotel room, with a king-sized bed and a bathroom.

Lying there in the dark, though, I quickly found I couldn't relax. Every time I closed my eyes I saw that threatening message dripping down the wall, and it made me shiver.

Alexis reached out and pulled me back up against him,

warm in the dark. "First thing in the morning, we'll hit the stores to replace our things," he said, like maybe I was a little girl who could be distracted with a shopping trip.

"What if they come back?" I sounded hoarse. All the tears I had not shed the last few hours broke in my voice.

"They won't."

"How can you be so sure?"

"Wack-a-doodle," he said. "Out to scare us, to make us run. Only way to handle people like that is to stand firm-- they scatter when they see they can't cow you."

I could hear the ring of truth in his words, truth hard-won through experience, but for me it wasn't that easy. I could remember a time in my own not-too-distant past when I put freaky events down to randomness, and I had been wrong. What if Alexis was wrong this time?

I laid awake, wide-eyed, the echo of a dead man's maniacal laugh ringing in my ears.

♫

We spent the next morning shopping. The hotel had given us toothbrushes and toothpaste, combs and brushes, soap and shampoo, deodorant and razors, but we still had almost two weeks of clothes to replace, including a concert tuxedo for Alexis. If we bought it today, the shop assistant told us, they would rush the adjustments to have it fitted in time for the concert.

All of our luggage, all of my makeup, even our shoes were gone. It was a good thing Alexis's first rehearsal with the Philharmoniker was scheduled for late afternoon, because it took us most of the day to feel like we had what we needed to make it comfortably through the next week, and then back home.

It was also a very good thing that Zwickau had such an incredible shopping district. Big, multi-level department stores and small specialty shops, all within easy walking distance, insured that we could find anything we wanted.

I never really thought of shopping as a particularly tiring activity, but by the time we made it back into the room, I could barely drag myself to the bed to flop down on it. Almost as soon as we walked in, it was time for Alexis to leave again.

"You sure you'll be all right here alone?" He slung his violin case over his shoulder and turned to regard me dubiously.

"Of course." In truth, that morning I would have felt very differently about being left alone. Now, I was too tired to care. "I'll get these new clothes to the hotel laundry. Maybe I'll take a nap."

"You do look like you could use one." He stood for a moment, looking around as though he was searching for a reason to stay. He didn't find one, though, so he came over and kissed me goodbye. "I suppose I will see you after rehearsal, then."

"I'll be here."

"See that you are." The serious way he said that gave me a chill. It reminded me unpleasantly of the previous evening.

By the time I recovered myself enough to respond, though, he was already gone.

I dropped my head back against the pillows. A nap really did sound good. But I figured I should at least try to get something worthwhile done.

I pulled all of the tags off of our new clothes and sorted them into plastic bags for the hotel laundry. It wasn't much of a chore, but my eyes were so heavy it seemed like a major accomplishment.

So I gave up and went to bed. I knew that taking naps at weird times of day wasn't doing much to help with my jet lag, but I was past caring. Before my head even hit the pillow, I was sound asleep.

It can be difficult to tell how long you have slept when you don't even dream. The nap I took that evening was a sleep too heavy for dreams, the kind of sleep I have only fallen into when I was profoundly exhausted. I slept like a rock, unmoving, and when the noise awoke me a couple of hours later, my brain was addled with sleep like a drug, and I was completely disoriented.

I couldn't remember for a long moment where I was, and it seemed to take me forever to work out that the jarring sound filling the room was the ringing of the telephone on the nightstand.

I rolled across the bed towards it. My limbs felt heavy, and I was clumsy and uncoordinated. "Hello?" My voice sounded as bleary and unfocused as I felt.

Ear-blistering static filled the line. I jerked the phone back, swearing. Even from a foot away, I could hear the noise. I could also hear something else breaking through the interference in fits and starts--a voice, female, heavily accented.

"...find you...with Alexis Brooks...warn you...get away..."

I stiffened. Even broken into bite-sized pieces, that sounded uncommonly like a threat. Was all this the work of a jealous fan? "Look here, I'm not afraid of you. Are you the coward who broke into our hotel room?" I shouted my question into the static, even though I couldn't see any way this person could hear me over that.

But she must have, because her reply came trickling back. "...worse than that...soon...get away from...Alexis Brooks...understand me?"

I understood all right. I understood that I was being threatened, and I slammed the handset back into the cradle hard enough to make the ringer bells jangle.

The nerve of these people! Alexis was right, the only way to deal with them was to show no fear. As if giant capital letters written in apparent blood were not enough, they had to call to make sure we got the message!

Well, I had gotten the message. And I was determined to stand strong against it. Because whatever misgivings I personally might have held about this trip, anyone could see that Alexis was having the time of his life. It was his first performance outside of Newton, Ohio in six years, and I wasn't going to let some anonymous bullies take it away from him. I couldn't even guess their reason for trying, but it didn't matter. It wasn't their decision to make.

I was too worked up to sleep now, and my mouth was bone-dry from my heavy, if tragically short, nap. I stomped into the bathroom and ran myself a drink of water into a heavy glass with the hotel logo on the side. The water did wonders for my mouth, but did little to cool my temper.

The phone rang again, a shrill, ear-splitting sound in the small room. I hurried over to it, trying my hardest to get a hold on myself. It was probably only Alexis calling to tell me he was on his way back. "Hello?"

There was no high-decibel white noise on the other end, which was an immediate relief.

"You have been warned."

The voice was male, and it seemed cultured. Every word was clipped, precise, and yet the accent was unmistakeably the same as the woman who had called before.

"What, can't you people take a hint? I've already told you, we aren't leaving!"

There was a short pause. "Very well. You will not be warned again."

The click that ended the call was as cold and efficient as the man himself had been.

I sank down onto the bed, the phone dead and forgotten in my hand, suddenly cold. That hadn't sounded so much like a threat.

It sounded like a promise.

I couldn't feel my hands. I couldn't seem to breathe. It didn't register with me when Alexis let himself into the room; I didn't realize I had tears on my face until he hurried over to kneel in front of me, brushing them away with his fingers. "Chrispen! What's wrong? What happened?" He glanced at the phone in my hands. "Bad news from home?"

I shook my head, staring at the telephone as though I had no idea what it was or what to do with it.

Alexis lifted the receiver from my hand and placed it back in the cradle, frowning. "I don't understand."

I took a deep, steadying breath. "It was a threat. The same people who trashed the suite. They want us to leave."

"Charming," he said dryly, and sat back on his heels.

"You said 'they'. There was more than one?"

"Two. A man and a woman."

"Did either of them sound familiar?"

I shook my head. "Not at all. They both had the same accent, though."

"Accent? You mean German?"

I thought about it. "I suppose it could be--I'm terrible with that kind of thing. But they didn't sound like everyone else here. They sounded more like your father, to me."

"Russian?" Alexis stood up and ran a hand through his hair. "I don't understand."

"Me either." I sighed. "But I guess crackpot vigilante fans come in all nationalities."

"I guess." He didn't sound convinced. "This seems odd, though. Something about this isn't screaming 'crackpot fan' to me anymore, Chrispen, and I can't put my finger on what it is. But I think you should come to rehearsals with me from now on."

"I thought they were closed rehearsals."

"They are. But you're coming anyway." Alexis scooped up the telephone receiver and punched the zero button on the base as though it had personally offended him. I could hear the bells jingle again. "Hello? Good evening. Yes, this is Alexis Brooks. I would like you to hold all calls for this room, please. Yes. No, there's no need to screen them. Just don't let any of them through. Right. For our entire stay. Thank you."

I watched him hang up the phone with a sort of dread. Of course blocking our calls made sense. It was the logical thing to do, and it had to be done. But I knew one thing for certain, and looking at the grim set of his face, I wondered if Alexis knew it, too: This would slow them down.

But it wouldn't stop them.

♪

The letter was delivered by courier, right to our hotel room. It had no return address, no marking we could find to tell us where it had come from. It was handwritten, and right to the point.

> Mr. and Mrs. Brooks,
>
> I did try to warn you. The vandalism of your suite was regrettable. I do hope that you will simply return home now; it would be most prudent. I beg you, go back to your home and forget every thing that has occurred in Zwickau while you still can.
>
> Anya

Wilhelm Braun shook his head, clucking to himself. "Clearly it is as I have told you. I do not know who this person could be, but we will submit this to the police. I would advise you not to accept any further deliveries."

I nodded. We had figured that much out for ourselves-- this note seemed much like the phone call--calm, polite, and full of simple pleading. But I was disturbed by the last line.

...while you still can...

That last line was neither polite nor pleading.

It was a threat.

I couldn't bear to leave the room so soon after that. We ordered in room service, and ate dinner piled up together in the king-sized bed, watching the news go by on a local channel in a language we didn't understand. It was cozy and fun, and it was the happiest I had been since we left home.

Until they showed a picture of the Hotel Sachsen Zwickau, and a publicity shot of Alexis, and we didn't need to speak German to know what the anchor was talking about. Some thoughtful person had leaked photos of our destroyed suite, which played in a montage under the brisk, efficient voice-over.

I stared, unable to look away, glued to the screen by my growing horror. There on the television screens of millions of viewers were detailed color photographs of my ripped undergarments littering the floor, my shredded clothes hanging off of vandalized furniture. I could see the box of tampons I had brought from home, torn open, its contents strewn about the room like demented confetti.

How could something so completely cold and impersonal feel like such an intimate invasion?

Alexis glanced at my frozen face and abruptly switched off the television. "Chrispen, are you all right?"

I moved my half-empty plate to the nightstand. "I'm not hungry."

Alexis put his own dinner aside on his nightstand and pulled me close. "Oh, honey. I know this is no fun. But take a deep breath and try to step back. That was not about you, and it wasn't about me. It never is. It's about raising ratings, or selling papers, or moving magazines."

"Magazines?" My stomach lurched unpleasantly. "You mean this is in the *tabloids?*"

He shrugged helplessly. "I did try to warn you before you married me. The ride isn't always going to be easy."

"No, no, it isn't that." I waved a hand, brushing that line of discussion away. "I just need a moment to accept this."

"It isn't personal," he reiterated. "You've got to remember that, because we're going to see worse."

I nodded. I could well believe it--I remembered only too clearly some of the tabloid headlines after Alexis's first wife had been murdered, and he had been accused. I swallowed hard. "Don't they think we have any right to privacy at all?"

"No," he said simply. "I'm sure you've heard the argument that privacy is forfeited for fame."

"But that's not fair! None of those people would stand for being treated like this."

"Maybe not, but they don't have the perks we do."

I didn't buy that. But as I opened my mouth to argue my point, Alexis leaned over and kissed me and I forgot all about arguing. My mouth melted against his and I reached up, pulling him closer. The evening, it seemed, would be better spent exploring some of those perks.

♬

I sat on the bed the next morning, flipping through the concert program Alexis had brought home from the rehearsal, while he shaved in the little mirror over the sink.

"You're going to laugh at me," I said, "but I never even realized Schumann wrote a violin concerto."

"Tsk, tsk," he chided. "What does a Juilliard education get you these days?"

He was making strange faces in the mirror, trying to shave around his mouth. I laughed at him, and he stuck his tongue out at me.

"I don't think it's that surprising," I said defensively. "It can't be too popular, judging from its nickname. Do they really call it the Lost Concerto?"

"Some do." Alexis rinsed his razor in the sink. "If you mentioned a lost concerto, and you were talking about the violin, I don't know what other concerto I would think you meant."

"Lots of drama around it," I mused, scanning the notes in the program. "Joachim actually left instructions in his will that it should not be performed until one hundred years after Schumann's death?"

"He did indeed. If you ask me, he was trying to save Schumann's reputation. He always felt the concerto wasn't Schumann's best work, that his mental problems showed through in it too clearly."

"Mental problems," I echoed. I remembered my own flash of madness at the Zwickauer Mulde. Had Schumann ever considered drowning himself in that river? I shivered.

Alexis looked at me sharply. "But perhaps that conversation is a bit...pedantic for right now."

"Perhaps," I said, holding out the program. "These notes are as dry as week-old bread. Who wrote this?"

"I wrote that, thank you very much." He took the program and swatted me with it.

I laughed. "Sorry, Professor. I didn't mean to hurt your feelings. How can I make it up to you?"

"See me after class," he said, and he leaned over and

kissed me.

I closed my eyes and kissed him back. The world seemed to swirl around me in a haze. I lost my balance and fell backward onto the bed, dragging Alexis with me.

"Hmm." He trailed kisses down the side of my neck, laughing low in his throat. "Is this an invitation?'"

I tousled his hair, and ruffled it through my fingers. "I suppose that would be one way to spend the morning."

He rolled away from me onto his side, propping his face in his hand to regard me. "And here I thought you wanted to do some sight-seeing."

I considered it. "Sight-seeing... Maybe I saw enough of Zwickau yesterday morning."

"Maybe." He traced his fingers over my lips. "But wouldn't it be embarrassing if the maid came to make the bed and we were in it?"

"That's what the 'do not disturb' sign is for, silly!" I slugged his arm and got up off the bed. "But I can see you aren't going to take yes for an answer. What did you have in mind?"

"Don't be a grump. There's a whole city out there we haven't seen, a hundred thousand people we haven't met. I'm sure we'll find something to do."

One of the fabulous things about Zwickau is how very easy it is to get around without a car. We left the Mercedes parked in front of the room and rode a hotel shuttle into town. The shuttle dropped us off in the market square, by the town hall. From there, we found a combination of walking and taking the public tram system could get us wherever we wanted to go.

Standing in the main market square of Zwickau was like being in a postcard--a living, moving postcard. I stood on the cobblestone and turned in a slow circle, trying to take it all in. The clean, whitewashed look of buildings contrasted sharply with deep wooden trim and fiery red rooftops, and farther away were blues, and greens, all against the gray paving stones below. Every color seemed to pop, more vibrant and alive in this moment than any before. Behind it all, a church spire climbed the morning sky, towering over all of us.

"It's gorgeous, isn't it?" Alexis's voice came from behind me.

I turned to face him, and found him sitting on the edge of a large sculpted fountain, waiting while I soaked in the sights. He was smiling at me like nothing could ever go wrong in the world again, happy and relaxed, and the sight of him there surrounded by all that dazzling color was sensory overload. I pulled out my cell phone and snapped his picture, unwilling to let go of the moment, ever.

"Absolutely gorgeous," I said, flipping the phone closed. "But what will they do when you get up from there?"

His grin broadened. "Why, thank you. But you don't need to do that."

"What, take your picture?"

"Use your cell phone." He stood up, reaching into the pocket of his slacks. "I picked up a disposable camera in the hotel gift shop, since ours was destroyed in the...you know."

"I know," I agreed flatly. Those guys had smashed anything electronic into millions of little pieces when they ransacked our hotel room. Just thinking about it seemed to cast a gray pall over the bright, beautiful market square.

I shivered, but it had nothing to do with cold.

Alexis stood next to me and slipped his arm around my waist. "Here's the camera," he said, pressing it into my hand. "Go crazy. We can always pick up another one."

I took him at his word. The square seemed made for photographing. I just hoped the vivid colors would pop on film the way they did right then, in person. And the buildings--would their charm convey in print? I fervently hoped so.

My favorite was the Gewandhaus, and I had high hopes for the pictures of it. The building had charmed me instantly, with its gleaming white finish, offset handsomely by rich wood trim and ornamentation. It was tall, with a steepled shape that appealed to me--and perhaps best of all, though it had originally served as a clothier's guild hall, these days it was a theater. Fluttering white banners on the front announced some of the upcoming productions.

The large statue of Robert Schumann on the other side of the square reminded me that I wanted to be sure to visit the museum that had been made of the house where he had been born. It was just down the street, so we headed that way.

The museum was arranged into the rooms of the house, roughly divided into periods of the composer's life. Robert Schumann and his wife Clara were both pianists. Several pianos were on display in the museum, but the one that called to me was the Andre Stein on which Clara had played her debut performance when she was nine years old. The cherry wood gleamed warmly, and I had never in my life wanted to play a piano so badly. Me! I had stumbled through a four-part arrangement of *The Star-Spangled Banner* competently enough to earn my Proficient rating, and had never looked back. I knew this piano was still used in performances, but I also knew it was a valuable antique that didn't belong in amateur hands like mine. Now Alexis, on the other hand, probably could have done it justice.

"You must really like this piano," he said, coming to stand beside me. "This is the third time you've come back to it."

"I can't help it." I shook my head, but I couldn't seem to look away from the instrument. "Nine years old. Nine, and debuting on a grand piano custom-commissioned for her. Can you imagine how good she must have been?"

"I've always heard she was very talented," Alexis said.

"Very talented? She was extraordinary! I wonder...I wonder how far she might have gone, if she hadn't married a man who overshadowed her...if she had been able to really tour, to pursue her career."

Alexis looked at me oddly. "She's still famous today--this piano isn't on display because it was Robert's, you know. I'd say she did all right."

"No, it's on display because it was *Robert Schumann's wife's.* Not because it was Clara Wieck's. Don't you see the difference? She never got to be Clara Wieck the famous pianist, because she was too busy being Clara Schumann the famous composer's wife!"

"Hmm. Well, I suppose you do have a point. Still, she chose to marry him. Maybe that famous pianist's life wasn't what she wanted. Who's to say she wasn't happy?"

I frowned, at the piano, at my inability to get my point

through to Alexis. How could she have known whether she wanted fame or not, when she never had the chance to pursue it, stuck in her husband's shadow?

My reflection gazed back at me from the polished surface of the piano, biting her lip and looking troubled. Who was to say, indeed?

Farther into town, we visited the magnificent Dom St. Marien, with its high vaulted ceilings and archways, and beautiful reliefs. It dwarfed and humbled us.

We found the nearby Priesterhauser to be a stark contrast to the richness of the church. Originally built as housing for the men of the church, the buildings had been restored as a testament to life in medieval times. It was like another world, climbing those narrow, steep wooden staircases, ducking through low doorways into tiny chambers, almost too small to properly call rooms. From the outside, the windows high in the roof of the buildings looked like watchful eyes, ever vigilant, looking out at the surrounding town.

And then we found that one of the buildings had been converted into a modern--and very good--microbrewery, complete with beer garden. It seemed a funny juxtaposition to me, but that may have been the effects of the rather strong brew I had selected.

I don't know if I've ever had more fun in my life than playing tourist with Alexis in Zwickau. Everything was new to us, and wonderful. I decided it was worth getting out of bed for after all. Alexis nearly spilled his ale laughing when I told him so.

By early afternoon, we had dropped off our camera at a one-hour photo lab who promised to deliver the photos to our hotel, and we were in Schwanenteich; Swan Pond. The park lived up to its name, with a huge glassy pond where swans floated by. We bought bratwurst and sauerkraut from a small stand and wandered on, eating and talking and enjoying the views. The park seemed deserted, until we came to a spot near the boat rentals where a man played accordion while a group of young acrobats performed. They had drawn a larger crowd than I would have thought possible.

We moved around the back toward the middle of the crowd and watched the show for a few minutes. They really were entertaining, but I found myself struggling to pay attention, their costumes blending into meaningless blurs of color. There was something I was missing here, something *important*. I just didn't know what it was.

It was nagging, frustrating, like an itch I could not scratch. I shifted my weight to my other foot and glanced quickly around, trying very hard to look casual about it.

Alexis looked at me suddenly. "What is it? What's wrong?" So much for casual.

There.

"That woman." I jerked my chin in her direction, off to my right, a bit closer to the performance than we were. Tall, statuesque, with blonde hair she had swept into an elegant updo. Dark, oversized sunglasses hid a lot of her face. "I think she's following us. I saw her at Schumann's house, and at the cathedral."

Alexis followed my gesture. He pulled off casual a lot better than I did. "Hmm." He frowned. "I haven't noticed her. Maybe she's just a tourist. Those are all very common tourist attractions."

"She must not get out much, for a tourist. Look how pale she is."

"All the more reason for a vacation," Alexis said. "I think you're just jumpy, after all that's happened."

I frowned, staring at the woman. If she turned around she'd probably think I had lost my mind. Alexis certainly seemed to. But I knew I was right. "Alexis, I'm sure about this. I'm telling you--"

Alexis was gone. While we had been talking, the show had ended, and that enormous crowd was dispersing all at once, and some of them in a hurry. Alexis had been swept abruptly into the moving crowd, and I found the woman had been shuffled away as well.

"Damn!" I stood there uncertainly in the torrents of moving people, wondering what I should do.

A large man in a dark suit with square-shaped sunglasses hurried past me, shouldering me backwards into someone else. I stumbled, caught myself, and turned to apologize. "Excuse me," I said reflexively, and gasped.

Standing in front of me was another man in a dark suit. He even had the same sunglasses, with the same square-shaped, mirrored lenses.

"It's nothing of consequence," he said, and time seemed to freeze. *I knew his voice!* I had heard it coldly threaten me on the hotel phone only the day before. But to meet him here, now--I couldn't seem to breathe properly.

"But are you lost?" he asked me, as though he hadn't noticed my discomfort. "You don't seem to be from around here. Perhaps it would have been wiser for you to just *go home."*

He looked at me over the top of his sunglasses, and my stomach went cold. *You will not be warned again...*this man was not here to threaten. He was here to follow through.

I knew I should run, but my feet were leaden.

The man's hand closed in a death grip on my arm, and he began dragging me toward the heavy trees behind the clearing, away from everyone else in the park.

Away from all the witnesses.

I knew that was bad, but I couldn't force myself to move. I stumbled stupidly along behind him. I couldn't even scream.

All at once the crowd parted, and I could clearly see the blonde woman, moving swiftly away from us.

The man in the suit saw her too. His hand tightened on me convulsively, and he froze.

"Irena!" he gasped.

Then he released me and dove into the shifting crowd after her.

I stood there in total shock, aware that I'd had a near miss.

But how exactly had my doom been averted? What on earth had just happened?

And what could I do about it?

"I don't understand," Alexis said. His tone was mild, but the way his knuckles clenched white on the steering wheel gave him away. I understood. My good mood had been hopelessly shattered as well. Our freshly developed photos were back in our hotel room, and neither of us had been able to summon up the enthusiasm or the desire to open them up and look at them. "What do these people want? Why are they after you?"

I shrugged helplessly. We had given up on sight-seeing after the episode in Schwanenteich, and had beaten it back to the hotel as fast as we could. The tram ran right up to Ballhaus Neue Welt, where Alexis had rehearsal with the Philharmoniker shortly, but neither of us were in the mood for public transportation right then. We were in the Mercedes, halfway between the hotel and Neue Welt.

"I don't know, Alexis. I've never seen that man before in my life. I don't know him from Adam. But I'd swear on my own grave that he is the one who called. And he seemed to know that woman. He called her Irena."

"So she is probably the woman who called first." Alexis threw up his hands in frustration. "But we don't know her either! This doesn't make *sense!*"

"Calm down," I said. "You need to keep your hands on the wheel. It isn't like you to get this worked up."

"Isn't like me," he echoed, clamping his fingers around the steering wheel. "It isn't like most strangers I've seen to threaten my wife, or to accost her and drag her off against her will. You're in danger, Chrispen, and I don't know how to protect you. I don't even understand the threat."

"Me either," I sighed. "The answers only lead to more questions. You're right. None of this makes any sense."

Alexis swung the car into a parking space and cut the engine. "Maybe we should just go home."

"What?"

"This is getting too dangerous. I can't handle you being at

risk, Chrispen, I just can't. We could be on a plane first thing in the morning, and--"

"No."

"Are you sure?"

"I'm positive." I shook my head. "You were right all along, Alexis, there's only one way to handle these people. I don't know what this is about, but if we give in to them now, their demands will only get bigger. We are not letting these people ruin your career."

"My career," Alexis said hollowly. "My career isn't worth this."

"Yes, it is!" I was surprised at my own intensity. "You're just starting to fly again. I'm not going to let them cage you up in Newton."

He reached out and brushed my cheek with his fingers. "It isn't me I'm worried about."

"I know that. Do you think I want to be stuck in that cage with you?"

Alexis laughed, but he didn't sound convinced. "Okay. You win. But at the first sign of any more trouble, we are high-tailing it back home."

"Of course," I said. "Now we had better get inside, or you are going to be late."

He looked at me a moment longer, like maybe he thought I was hiding something. Then he leaned over and brushed his lips against mine. "I love you, Chrispen."

Before I could answer, he got out of the car and went around to the back to retrieve his violin. I sat there a moment in the darkness, trying to figure out what had just happened. Should I have argued? Maybe it would have been best for us to just go home. But turning our backs on the career Alexis had spent his life building...I was not okay with that.

I couldn't figure anything out. I didn't have time, and I couldn't focus. The only thing I was certain of was the cold pit in bottom of my stomach.

And that didn't bode well for either of us.

If someone ever offers to send you a postcard from Zwickau, you could do worse than to ask for one of Ballhaus Neue Welt. I think it would be my first choice.

From the outside, the building might not bowl you over, with its covered entryway and prodigious use of glass, though I found it to be quite elegant. Inside, though--inside it will take your breath away. The concert hall was more beautiful than any building I had ever been in.

I sat in the hall during rehearsal, and they left the lights up for me. Sitting there among all the gorgeous archways-- over the main stage, around the box seats, lining the walls-- under that massive, sparkling chandelier--it was like nothing I had ever done before. I had to pinch myself. Of course Alexis was used to exotic locations and fabulous venues, but me? Just being there was a kind of system overload.

It made what might have been a mundane rehearsal into a spell-binding experience. A rehearsal with an outside soloist tended to be smoother than a regular rehearsal anyway, because you generally didn't bring the soloist in until the orchestra had their parts down. So there were less starts and stops than there might otherwise have been, and the music was nicer to listen to because of it.

The Philharmoniker Zwickauer was good, too, surprisingly so. Zwickau was a small city to support a symphony orchestra, but these people took their music seriously. This was an early rehearsal, only the second time Alexis had played with this group, but it was a joy to hear already. It was, I mused, more like a close duet than a solo. The conductor played his orchestra with the same nuance and feeling that Alexis put into his violin, and the result could sweep you away. Listening to a performance like that always made me kind of ache to play myself.

Sitting there with my hands feeling uncomfortably empty for the lack of a violin, I remembered Clara Wieck's piano, sitting lonely in the house where her husband was born. Maybe Alexis would have understood my point, if he had been stuck here in the empty hall, watching other people make music he could not join.

I thought Clara Schumann would have understood.

I lost track of myself, absorbed in the music and the surroundings, until a rude buzzing noise jerked me abruptly back to my senses.

A bit belatedly I remembered my cell phone, buried in my purse on the seat next to me. Thank heaven it was set to vibrate! I grabbed my purse and hurried back out to the lobby, digging for my cell phone as I walked. I hoped Alexis was too busy with his work to notice--it seemed to me the last thing he needed was something else to worry about.

The caller display on my phone showed "Unknown name, Unknown number."

I ground my teeth together. I'd had enough of this sort of thing to last me forever.

Still, ignoring them accomplished nothing. I flipped the phone open. "Hello?"

"Good evening." It was a woman's voice, accented but familiar. At least the connection was clear this time.

"Hello, Irena."

There was a short pause. "Where did you get that name?"

"It doesn't really matter. It's yours, isn't it?"

I could almost hear her thoughts, debating whether to give me that. "Yes," she said finally. "My name, as you have ascertained, is Irena Katarovski. It seems I have underestimated you."

"It seems you have underestimated several things. We are not leaving this place until our work here is done. I demand that you cease your harassment of us immediately, or I will take this to the authorities."

"No, wait!" She sounded desperate. "I have managed to stop the jamming, but we do not have much time to talk. You and Alexis must--"

"Nothing," I cut her off. "Alexis and I must do exactly nothing, except the job we came here to do."

"Please, just listen!"

"I've said all I'm going to say about this. Goodbye." I clicked my cell phone shut, frowning. Something about that had seemed off...

"What's up?"

I jumped; I hadn't realized there was anyone else in the room with me. I turned around to face Alexis, stuffing my phone back into my purse as I did. "Nothing."

He had his violin case slung over his shoulder; rehearsal must have ended. He glanced at my purse. "Another phone call?"

"Well, yes. I got her name this time. I think she's the woman we saw in Schwanenteich."

Alexis folded his arms. "I'll bet the woman in Schwanenteich was just an innocent bystander--it's just coincidence if their first names are the same. Doesn't it seem sort of careless to let herself be seen, if she's the one doing all of this?"

I frowned. "Well, yes...but this whole thing seems a little odd."

"More than a little, I'd say." Alexis took my arm and we started back towards the car. "Was the name familiar?"

"Not at all. Irena Katarovski."

"Katarovski," he mused. "I don't know of any Irena's, but there's something familiar about that last name." He considered it for a few steps. "Isn't there a politician in Russia with that last name? I think I remember him causing quite a stir."

"I don't know," I said. I didn't watch the news any more than I had to, and rarely read the newspaper beyond the concert reviews. "But I don't think it really helps us either way. What would a Russian politician want with us?"

"You're right," Alexis said bleakly. "I'm just glad we'll be leaving in a few more days, and none of this will be our problem any more."

"Famous last words," I quipped, and immediately wished I hadn't. Now that I thought about it, they really did kind of sound that way.

And that gave me a sinking feeling I didn't like at all.

I suppose it won't surprise you that I did not sleep well that night. I tossed and turned for hours, eaten up with worry about the things that had happened since we arrived in Zwickau. The more I worried, the more I worked myself up, and the more I worked myself up, the more I worried. It was a self-feeding cycle that seemed to have no end.

But even the most vicious cycle must give in to the demands of sleep in the end. It was well after two in the morning when I fell asleep, but I finally did. Even sleep offered no respite from my worries, however. My dreams were tortured and strange, tangled with images of a woman in over-sized sunglasses, of a man in a dark suit with a claw-like grip on my arm.

When I awoke, I could see sunlight peeking around the edges of the heavy drapes. The alarm clock on the nightstand showed 9:38 am.

9:38? How on earth had I managed to sleep so long? How had Alexis managed not to disturb me for that long? I rolled over.

The bed was empty. The room was dark. If it weren't for the extra luggage, and the second violin on the counter next to mine, it would have been hard to believe there was ever anyone else there.

I pushed myself into a sitting position against the pillows, and heard something crumple. A sheet of hotel stationery lay on Alexis's pillow, bearing a few lines of his neat, precise handwriting.

Gone to pick up tuxedo
Back soon

Enjoy your rest ☺
Love you -- A

Of course! I had forgotten--the men's store had agreed to rush the adjustments to his tux. It wouldn't be perfect, but it would fit well enough for the performance, and he could always have it properly fitted back home. He was supposed to pick it up that morning--half an hour before I even woke up, in fact--and I was supposed to go with him to make sure it looked all right; he claimed to have no eye for these things. Apparently he had decided to let me sleep instead. I must have bothered him more than I'd realized.

I was awake now, though. And he would be back before very much longer--the menswear shop was a very short trip by car. I twitched the curtain aside to verify--the Mercedes was not in its usual spot. He wouldn't be long at all.

I got dressed, fixed my hair and made myself presentable. I considered ordering in some breakfast, but I wasn't sure whether to order for one or two--I didn't want Alexis to come back and find me eating without him if he had waited on me. I started the coffeemaker instead, and figured I'd decide what to do about eating when he got there.

In the bright warm light of morning, I found the envelope of yesterday's pictures a lot more tempting. I smoothed out the big bed and spread the pictures on it, examining each one in turn. I had forgotten the sheer number of photos I had taken. They were good though--they seemed to embody not just the individual sights we had seen, but the spirit of fun and adventure that had permeated the better part of the day.

I stood back and regarded the pictures as a group, pleased with the effect the vivid colors had when they combined into a somewhat random whole. It was oddly pleasant to survey that whole mass, pick out a single photo to examine closely, then take in the formless whole again.

I was enjoying the chaotic blur of all those pictures jumbled together when I realized with a start that the blonde woman--Irena Katarovski--was in my picture of the outside of the Schumann House, one of a handful of strangers apparently wandering by.

A cold prickle crawled over my scalp. I *knew* I had seen her before Schwanenteich! I sat down gingerly on the edge of the bed and gave each of the pictures a closer inspection, this time ignoring the subjects and examining everything I had not meant to photograph.

I found Irena inspecting a bronze relief of the Virgin Mary at the Dom St. Marien, her back to the camera. She was in the beer garden, hiding her face behind those huge sunglasses and drinking something a good deal darker than either Alexis or I had ordered.

I knew she had been at these places--hadn't I told Alexis as much? But how closely must she have been shadowing us, to show up in our pictures of every place we had been? Was it deliberate--was the woman taunting us?

Most unsettling of all was the picture I found among my photographs of the Priesterhäuser. The eye-shaped window dormers had fascinated me, and I had taken a picture of one, as close up as I could get it.

In the window a man in a dark suit and sunglasses was clearly visible.

My creep-out threshold had just been crossed. I stuffed the pictures back into the envelope and resolved not to look at them again until I showed Alexis what I had found, when he came back.

I broke out my violin and took advantage of the downtime to get some practice in. I decided to have a go at the Schumann concerto myself--it would be more interesting than any of the music in my case; it was full of pieces I had already played.

With my violin and a hotel mug, I worked my way through the concerto and the coffee. The Schumann Violin Concerto felt rather scattered to me, and a bit difficult to get a handle on. It felt like a concerto that wanted to be a symphony. It would have been easy to set it aside unfinished.

And yet...I couldn't quite do that. There were places where something melodic and soaring broke through, something I could not resist. And every time I played one of those passages I fell in love with Schumann's Lost Concerto; I felt like I really got it on a level deeper than the notes printed on the page.

I finally finished, and put the music and my violin away. I hadn't had a good practice since leaving the States, and it was amazing what it did for my mood. I took my empty cup over for a refill, and--

Empty? The whole pot was gone already?

I stared at it in dumb-founded surprise. How long had I been at this?

I turned to look at the clock, and for a moment I couldn't seem to make sense of what I was seeing. I had been practicing for over three hours.

It was 1:24 in the afternoon.

Where was Alexis?

I dropped into a chair by the little table, my heart suddenly racing. He should have been back hours ago! A parade of horrors flashed through my mind; the twisted metal of an automobile accident, perhaps, or the wildly scattered clothing of a torrid affair, or the squealing brakes of an out-of-control car striking a pedestrian. Maybe he'd been mugged. Or maybe--

I fought against the rising black wave of panic. This was crazy; there was no reason to believe anything terrible had happened. There had to be a perfectly harmless explanation. And freaking out wouldn't help anyone.

I pawed through my purse for my cell phone, clumsy in my haste. My hands shook--it took me three tries to dial Alexis's number from the contact list.

There was no answer.

I was losing faith in my harmless explanations. I was in a foreign country, with no car, no friends, and my husband was missing.

With trembling fingers I picked up the hotel phone and dialed the office number the hotel security manager had left us.

♫

I don't think Wilhelm Braun knew quite what to make of me. I was incoherent and my story didn't make much sense. I'm not sure whether it was to protect me from foul play or because he suspected me of foul play, but he wrote a report, called the hotel manager, put me in his car, and drove me to the American consulate in Leipzig.

I don't remember much of that drive. My mind raced, pacing the confines of my situation like a tiger in a cage, but I sat stone still with my purse perched on my knees. I hoped against hope that my cell phone would ring, that Alexis would ask why I had gone running off without him. But I knew it wouldn't happen. There was just no conceivable way that he would be gone this long and not contact me, if contact was humanly possible.

Alexis, where are you?

A sudden chirp from inside my purse commanded my complete attention the second it happened--my cell phone receiving a text message.

I pawed it out of my purse and flipped it open, breathless with sudden anticipation. I was wracked with hope so potent it hurt.

The letdown when I saw the message displayed on the little screen was painful, too.

I can help you. --I.K.

I clicked the phone shut and shoved it back in my purse, blinking back sudden tears. I had really thought it would be Alexis.

I can help you. Yeah, right. As if there was a chance I would cooperate with the person behind all of this. What did she want with us? What could possibly be worth all this?

I didn't care. Bringing in the American Embassy would be like calling in the cavalry, and I couldn't wait. They would end this nightmare. I knew it.

I didn't realize the car had stopped until Mr. Braun turned to face me, clearing his throat uneasily. "Your cellular phone, Frau--you will not be able to enter the embassy with it."

I stared blankly at him. I recognized the words, but there seemed to be no possible way they could apply to me. I couldn't give up my cell phone; it was my only tie to Alexis.

"If you would like," he said, "I will keep it in the car while I wait for you."

I felt a rush of gratitude as I passed him the phone. "Thank you. But...why are you doing this for me?"

He couldn't quite seem to look me in the eye. "Your husband, Frau. I have been a fan for many years. So I do for you what I can. He loved you very much."

I was halfway to the consulate building before it hit me.

Why did he speak of Alexis in the past tense?

♫

If you have never had to convince an official that a grown man has disappeared because something bad happened, I sincerely hope you never have the pleasure.

"Here's the thing," Mark Staples said, flipping a ballpoint pen over in his fingers, clicking it open and shut. "When an adult, responsible, married man gets into his car and doesn't come back, it's usually because he doesn't want to."

"What are you saying?" I wasn't sure what I had expected from the consulate, but this wasn't it. I had given this man behind the Mark Staples nameplate my long and somewhat rambling account of events, but it had been clear he was only paying half attention.

Mark shrugged. "Maybe he decided marriage didn't suit him."

"Wait--are you saying my husband, married to me less than a year, *ran away?* To get away from me?"

"You'd be surprised how often it happens." This guy made me like him less every time he opened his mouth. "Look, this Alexis, he's a pretty famous guy, right? Lots of fans, recognized everywhere he goes? Maybe he decided a life like that is better enjoyed flying solo. I know I wouldn't want a dame hanging on my arm if it was me. Not the same one all the time, anyway. No offense," he said, tipping his pen in my direction. "But you want to know why a man would hit the road, you've got to think like a man."

"That doesn't make any sense." I scrubbed at my eyes with the heels of my hands. "What about his violin? Why would a man who makes his living as a violinist leave his violin behind?"

"Collateral damage. It was worth it to him to be free. Violins can be replaced."

I stared at him. I didn't know how to reason with someone like that--all the unfathomable hours spent finding just the right instrument, the hundreds of thousands of dollars involved in the purchase, the untold hours of bonding--anyone who would suggest with a straight face that a man would leave that behind just to get away from his wife could not be taken seriously.

"Look," I finally said, "what about the harassment, the trashed room, the phone calls? I have a name. I know who is behind it."

"You have a name?" He sat up straighter. "By all means, tell me. The police are liable to tell you the same thing I did, but with a name maybe we can convince them to investigate."

"Irena Katarovski."

The pen clattered onto his desk. "Run that by me one more time?"

"Katarovski. Irena Katarovski. Tall, blonde, early thirties. She's Russian."

He laughed a strangled laugh. "Russian. 'She's Russian,' says the lady." He sat back in his chair. "I'll be frank with you, Mrs. Brooks, if I was you I would be on the next plane home, and no joke."

"What?"

"Katarovski. Katarovski! You mean you don't know the name?"

"Russian politician, right?"

"Well, sort of." He shook his head. My ignorance was apparently astounding. "Petrov Katarovski is a great-grandson of Stalin, and very proud of it. His platform is a return to the golden days of the Soviet Union through a return to the policies of his dear great-grandpappy--purges, population transfers and all. A return to Stalinism...I don't want to use the term enemy of the state, but yeah, he is."

"Where does Irena fit into all this?"

"Hang me if I know," he said, "and hang me and shoot me if I care. The Katarovski's are bad people, Mrs. Brooks, dangerous people. If your husband is mixed up with them, you had better get yourself home before you meet a sticky end."

I stared at him.

"In fact," he said, turning abruptly to the computer beside him and typing ninety miles an hour, "I may be able to pull a few strings and...yes!"

He turned away from me and made a phone call,

speaking quickly and too quietly for me to hear.

"We're off." He hung up and stood abruptly out of his chair, taking my arm and hauling me along with him toward the entrance. "You're very lucky--this is way outside what the embassy does, but...well, a few people owe me some favors, and with the Katarovski's involved...don't worry. We'll get you home safe."

As soon as we came out of the consulate building, Wilhelm Braun came running up to me, in time to catch the end of Mark's words. "Your phone," he said, pressing it into my hands. "I wish you the best." He crossed himself, and hurried back to his car.

"Does he know the Katarovski's are involved in this?" Mark asked.

I shook my head. I was getting pretty tired of hearing him say that name.

He frowned. "I'm afraid that man thinks you are involved in your husband's disappearance."

"Excuse me?"

"It's probably best you are leaving. He will report to the local police, and you might have found yourself in an uncomfortable position, had you stayed. It's lucky he brought you here."

I didn't know how to answer. Things were moving so fast, and nothing made sense. My life seemed to be moving entirely around other people's whims, and my head was spinning.

A cab pulled to a stop in front of us. Mark held the door open for me. "Someone will meet you at the airport," he told me, taking my arm and helping me into the car in a manner that felt more like pushing me into the car. "Don't worry."

The door slammed shut with the finality of a death knell.

♪

Mark's friends must have owed him big. The cab driver got me to the Leipzig International Airport in record time, and refused all offers of payment. No sooner had I stepped out of the car than a short man in a suit scurried up to me. He wore round, wire-framed glasses and carried an airline ticket folder in his hands. "Mrs. Brooks?"

I looked at him blankly a moment before it sank in that I was expected to respond. "Yes--yes, I'm sorry, I'm not all here right now."

"It's quite all right, ma'am." He held out the little folder, and I took it as if I had never seen plane tickets before. "Your plane leaves in half an hour--you should have time, if you hurry." He stepped back, like he was anxious to be disassociated from me. "Good luck, ma'am."

"Thank you," I said absently, and watched him hurry away.

Abruptly, for the first time since I picked up the phone in the hotel room, I found myself in charge of my own destiny.

I stood there at the crossroads, staring at the paths I could take.

On the one hand: home, safety, my job and even my mother. The logical choice, the safe choice, the choice my country would have me make.

On the other hand there was nothing but fear, danger, and uncertainty. Collusion with my enemies, the enemies of my country, in a last desperate attempt to save the man I loved more than life.

I stared at the tickets in my hand, the tangible proof of the path to safety laid before me. I tried to imagine taking it; tried to imagine boarding that plane without Alexis, flying home alone, and living by myself in his house in Newton, never seeing him again. Living the rest of my life as if I had never known what it is to love, and to have that love returned.

Before I knew what I was doing, I tore the plane tickets in half. After I knew what I was doing, I tore them in half again, and again, and again, until the pieces were too tiny for me to grip.

Then I tossed them all up over my head like confetti, and while the tiny fragments flipped and fluttered down to the ground, I marched off toward the car rental counters.

I was racing back towards Zwickau in a rented Audi A4, as fast as I thought I could get away with, when my cell phone rang.

I had rather expected it. I felt more rational and in control than I had all day--I had already called the Hotel Sachsen Zwickau and arranged to have our violins held there until we could come for them.

I picked up the phone and flipped it open without looking at it. "Hello, Irena."

"You did not listen to your countrymen."

"I can't leave Alexis." I had brought my best tough act with me, but my voice broke anyway.

"You may regret it."

I took a deep breath. "Listen, they gave me the scare story about your family, but--"

"Whatever they have told you is true. You may not live long enough to regret your decision, if you stay."

"I don't care. I'll spend the rest of my life regretting it if I go. I will not leave without Alexis."

There was a long pause, then she released a pent-up sigh. "Good girl. I am not your enemy, Chrispen Brooks, and I will help you as much as I can. That they have taken him-- this is not good. We must move quickly."

"Is Alexis still alive?" My voice quavered; I clenched my hands on the steering wheel, trying to keep myself together.

She paused for a second. "He is. I did not have a hand in taking him. But I know where he is held. Together we will get him back."

"Thank you." My instinct was to ask for some assurance that she could be trusted, but I knew it was far too late for that. "What do you want from me?"

"I ask only that you listen," she said, "when the time comes."

"Tell me what to do."

"Gewandhaus," she said. "There is a fountain nearby, in the hauptmarket. Can you be there in half an hour?"

I remembered the town hall, and the fountain in front. "Can do." I clicked the phone shut and tossed it onto the passenger seat, pushing the Audi even faster.

I supposed Irena was right; this may not have been the most rational decision I had ever made. This was dangerous; very high risk with little chance of success. And if this "enemy of the state" talk was true--and I had no reason to believe that it wasn't--then going home could soon cease to be an option for me. I could come out of this without Alexis, without a home, without even a violin to support myself--if I even came out of this at all. No sane person would gamble with stakes that high.

But I had known all that when I made my decision.

I gritted my teeth and drove a little faster.

The Gewandhaus was right next to the Zwickau city hall in the main market square. It was a theater these days, but its name--garment-house--reflected its origin as a guild hall for tailors. It was said that the intricate design work in the front gable end contained a secret that would allow journeymen to prove they had visited Zwickau.

Right out in front was a beautiful concrete fountain surrounded by benches, depicting children dancing in a circle.

The area was sort of out-of-the-way compared to the shopping districts and some of the bigger tourist attractions, but it was gorgeous and there were always plenty of people milling around.

It was a very good meeting place for a couple of people with no wish to draw unnecessary attention to themselves.

I felt a pang as soon as I stepped into the picturesque market square; this was one of the places I had visited with Alexis only the day before. In fact, I remembered taking a picture of him sitting on the edge of the fountain I was now headed for.

Without pausing to engage my better judgment, I pulled the picture up on my phone.

It knocked the breath out of me. I missed a step and stumbled to a clumsy halt, my eyes brimming with stinging tears. Alexis beamed out of the little screen at me, happy and excited and so, so full of love. I had been acutely aware of his absence all day, but at that moment it felt like a physical hole in my chest, and I didn't see how I could carry on.

Quitting was not an option, though. There was only one way I was going to make it through this, and that was to remember that whatever I did, I did for Alexis. He was still alive. It was up to me to keep him that way.

I jammed the phone back in my purse and moved quickly toward the fountain, my resolve restored. Irena had to be around here somewhere, and she should be easy to spot.

When I did see her, I nearly stumbled again. It gave me a nasty turn to see her sitting on the edge of the fountain, smiling at me from behind her big sunglasses, in exactly the same spot and pose as Alexis in the picture I had just put away. How did she know? Had she been following us even then?

I had my reservations about trusting her, about accepting her help. But what choice did I have? If she knew where Alexis was, she held all of the cards. Whether I believed she had no hand in this or not, I had no choice but to work with her.

"You made it." She turned away, not looking at me when she said it; she might have been talking to anyone.

"You sound surprised."

Irena shrugged. When she did it, the motion was somehow graceful. "You might have changed your mind. It is not a very wise thing, what we are doing."

"I already told you; I can't leave him. I'll go home when Alexis does, and not before."

"I admire your loyalty. Alexis Brooks must be quite a man, to inspire such dedication."

"He is." I paused. "You reminded me of him, sitting there just the way he did yesterday. I don't believe that was accidental. What are you playing at?"

Irena suddenly turned to face me, and that instantly put me on my guard. I don't know what I expected--perhaps a flood of Russian invective--but what she did was calmly reach up and remove her sunglasses.

I gasped and stepped back from her.

"What? What is it?" Her tone was mild, but she was leaning toward me expectantly.

"Nothing," I said quickly, waving my hands in front of me. "Nothing--I'm sorry, I just--for a moment you reminded me of someone else. It's nothing."

"I see," Irena said, but she seemed sad. She turned away from me again, and as the light on her face changed, the effect I had seen faded.

But for a moment, her eyes had looked just like Alexis's.

"Turn right here," Irena directed. "Okay, pull over there. We'll have to park and walk from here on in."

I guided the Audi into the spot she indicated. We were in a part of Zwickau I was utterly unfamiliar with, and quite frankly did not like the look of. I sat in the quiet for a moment, regarding the sunset over the unfamiliar skyline. "Where are we going?"

"Pulverturm," Irena said. "It is a tower still standing from the city's original medieval fortifications. It was used for gunpowder storage at one time...but it has been unused for many years."

"Sounds charming," I said, and got out of the car.

Irena stepped out as well, and started leading me right into the part of this I liked the least--the giant, blocky concrete buildings covered with small, dark windows that stared into the oncoming night like hollow eyes.

"I don't like this place," I said, surprised to find myself whispering. "What are these buildings? They don't seem like part of Zwickau at all."

"Plattenbauten," Irena said shortly. "It's a German word for buildings constructed of pre-fabricated concrete slabs, like these. They are Communist-era apartment blocks."

"Communist-era? Zwickau was part of East Germany?"

"Yes. What you see here are the scars." Irena sounded sad, particularly for someone whose father was busily pushing for a return to those ideals.

On the other side of the plattenbauten, completely out of place with the surroundings, was a rock wall, ending in a two-story tower that was round on the side facing out from the city, and flat on the side facing back towards town. In medieval times, it would have been a formidable defense. Now, though, it was completely dwarfed by the cookie-cutter Socialist apartment blocks around it.

I found that kind of scary. Especially considering my current company.

The old-fashioned wooden door to the tower sported a high tech electronic lock with a number pad. Irena paused and slipped a mean-looking Beretta compact pistol out of her purse. Its nickel finish gleamed in the low light, and clearly said it meant business.

She tapped in a series of numbers on the keypad--18121878.

"How do you know that?" I whispered.

"Stalin's birthday," she hissed back. "Simple when you know who is in charge here."

She seemed to be right. With a barely perceptible click, the electronic lock disengaged.

Irena turned to regard me, her white face tight with fear. "Be careful. I do not know what awaits us here."

That fear--I did not believe Irena was a good enough actress to fake that. She seemed far more trustworthy here, pale and frightened, than she had when she was calm and confident in the main market.

We stepped into the silent wooden darkness of the tower, where the air was heavy with unfamiliar, earthy smells. The blackness surrounding us was absolute; I could only see the curved staircase hugging the rounded wall of the tower because of the warm light spilling partway down it from the second floor.

"Welcome!" The cultured, Russian-accented voice was familiar, and a cold fist clenched around my heart when I heard it. Was this his plan all along? Had he only taken Alexis because he let me go? "Come upstairs, if you please. Do not keep us all waiting."

Irena started to move towards the stairs, but I held out a hand to stop her. She looked at me questioningly, and I held a finger to my lips, lifted the Beretta out of her hand, and motioned her back into the darkness.

Irena disappeared into the shadows across from the stairs. I had a hunch it would be better if she remained undetected; an ace in the hole of sorts.

I took a deep, steadying breath, and started up the wooden stairs. They creaked loudly, as if announcing my progress to the men waiting above.

Upstairs, I found two familiar men in dark suits. They wore their mirrored sunglasses even in here, and they both held guns that looked like they could eat the Beretta's lunch. And both weapons were pointed squarely at me.

Lanterns flickered here, and I saw a long, low table that turned my stomach to look at very closely. From where I stood, I could make out short, stout metal pipes, brass knuckles, and even syringes with needles and assorted vials. There were matches that must have been four inches long--some of which had been burned down almost all of their length. A short, vicious-looking leather whip lurked on the end of the table, waiting to serve who-knew-what dreadful purpose. The table was bone-chilling.

But that wasn't the most disturbing thing in the room.

On the far side of the room, beside one of the suits, hanging from the wall by manacles that dug into his wrists, was a beaten and bloodied Alexis. His ruined concert tuxedo hung off of him, cut through in places by something that looked as though it had cut him as well.

He was completely limp; he didn't even have the strength to hold up his head. If I hadn't heard his ragged breathing, I would have thought he was dead.

It made my blood boil, seeing him like that, knowing that

these two men had done this thing to him. I wanted nothing in the world more than to open fire on both of them, even though I knew I would never get out of there alive if I did.

The Beretta twitched in my hand as though it had similar ideas. The suit next to Alexis caught the motion and frowned. "Please, place your weapon on the floor."

Someone capable of such appalling brutality pretending to be gracious set my teeth on edge. I hated him for his fake politeness, on top of everything else. I knelt down and carefully laid the Beretta on the wooden floor. So much for that advantage; I should have just left it with Irena.

"May I see my husband?" The words had a bite; I had to force them past my clenched jaw.

"Certainly," the suit replied in his falsely gracious manner, "after you answer some questions. Your dear husband, as you can see, was less than cooperative. I do encourage you not to repeat his mistakes."

I swallowed hard and nodded. "I'll tell you anything." The words burned, but they were true.

"Smart girl," he chuckled. His laugh sounded nasty, and it made my skin crawl. He jabbed an elbow roughly into Alexis's side. "You must be so proud."

Alexis stiffened, his back arching painfully against the stone wall, groaning in agony. He managed to lift his haggard face to look at me. "Chrispen..." The word was harsh and rasping, his voice a hollow shell of its usual self.

"Hush now, and let your lovely wife do the talking. How do you know Irena Katarovski?"

"I don't," I said. "I only know the name. She told me when she called me yesterday."

"Mmm. And where is she now?"

"I don't know." My voice quavered. I could only hope he would attribute it to nerves.

"I see." He shoved his gun into a shoulder holster, then closed his jacket and began to pace in front of Alexis, his hands behind his back. That pacing struck me as ominous. "You want to be careful now, Mrs. Brooks. We do not believe in second chances. How did you come here tonight, if Irena is not with you?"

I held up my cell phone. "She called me earlier and told me to come here."

Suit Number One nodded at Suit Number Two and gestured at the phone. "Check it." All of the polite veneer was peeled from his voice; it had all the charm now of grating metal.

Suit Number Two stepped forward and took my phone, rapidly pushing buttons. "It checks. There is a call here from Katarovski."

Suit Number One said something in Russian I could only assume would have gotten his mouth washed out with soap if his mother had heard him. "I see. Irena is cagier than I had imagined. I did expect her to come here tonight herself. She is also far more willing to gamble with your lives than I had realized." He tossed a small keyring with two keys at my feet. "Get him down from there. We are taking a little ride." He picked up the Beretta and shoved it into his waistband, then stood back and waited.

I can't print the things I was thinking about him. But I had what I wanted most at that moment: a way to release Alexis. I scooped up the little keys and hurried over to him.

Alexis looked even worse up close. "Oh my God, oh my God," I said over and over under my breath as I struggled to unlock the manacles with my shaking hands. "Oh, my God." I couldn't seem to stop myself. What had they *done* to him?

He slumped to the floor as soon as the cuffs were open. I hauled him up to lean on me in something approaching a standing position, alarmed at how unresisting he was. "Chris," he said, and the word was hardly more than a breath. "Am I dead? Are you an angel?"

"Hush, now," I said, squeezing the words past a painful lump in my throat. "No one is going to die."

But I held onto him even tighter when I said it.

Suit Number One laughed his nasty chuckle and started down the stairs. "Come now, boys and girls. We've got a long way to go."

I followed him down the stairs, supporting Alexis in an awkward, painful half-shuffle, fantasizing about pushing the monster down the stairs. If only Suit Number Two wasn't right behind us.

We hobbled across the first floor in the dark. I prayed fervently that Irena would make a move before Suit Number One got out the door--I really did not want to find out what he had in mind for us.

I heard a sudden, strangled sound behind me, cut off before I could figure out what it was. It didn't matter; I had to assume Irena had acted. If I was wrong, we would all be dead.

"Hold on, Alexis," I whispered, and released him.

Three quick steps forward--Suit Number One was just turning around in annoyance to find out what had happened. I jerked the Beretta out of his waistband and jammed it into his belly before he could reach for his shoulder holster under his jacket.

"Hands up," I said, "unless you want to see how fast I can empty this clip."

He put his hands on his head, but the look he gave me made my blood run suddenly cold.

I backed up a couple of steps, keeping the pistol trained on Suit Number One, steadier than I had thought myself capable of.

Irena jerked something away from Suit Number Two and let him fall--I realized with a shock that she had strangled him with the long leather shoulder strap of her purse. She looked over and saw me.

"Kill him!" she gasped, her eyes wide.

Suit Number One let out a ragged, derisive laugh. "You misplace your faith in these dogs, Irena. We will hunt them down--whether I live or die. She won't kill me. She hasn't got the spine. The woman is soft, like her soft, pathetic husband."

He straightened up and spat a wad of something unspeakable at my battered Alexis, who was supporting himself in a wavering stand, both hands on the wall.

The Beretta jumped in my hands, the sharp report painfully loud in the small space. I remembered the leather whip and the table, and the cuts in Alexis's tuxedo, the wounds he sustained that bled even now, and the pistol cracked again. I thought about the syringes, the matches, the pipes and the brass knuckles, the way Alexis couldn't stand without assistance, how he had seriously believed himself to be dead, from the things this man had done to him.

The next thing I was aware of was the hollow click of an empty clip.

"Chrispen." A gentle hand fell on my shoulder. I turned, startled, to find Alexis there--I had no idea how he had managed to stagger over to me, how he was even standing upright.

"Alexis," I said, and my voice broke, and I began to cry. "Oh, God, Alexis..."

He gathered me into his arms and I sobbed against his chest, Irena's gun still warm in my hands.

Thirteen.

That's how many rounds a Beretta 84FS Cheetah magazine holds. That's how many bullets flew between the life and death of one man in the Pulverturm.

Of course, he was a horrible, horrible man. I knew that well enough. And I had very nearly lost Alexis. If that man had made it out of there with us, we would both have been dead.

Still, it shook me. Thirteen. It kept rolling around in my head as Irena recovered Alexis's cell phone from the body and jammed it into my purse, as we escaped the Pulverturm, as I helped Alexis into the backseat of the Audi, as Irena drove us away.

Thirteen.

Finally my grim reverie was broken when Irena spoke, the first words any of us had said since we got in the car. "Does anyone need anything before we leave Zwickau?"

"Yes," I said. My voice sounded unnaturally loud in my

own ears. "I have to get medical supplies for Alexis."

Irena nodded and looked back at the road. It seemed none of us felt much like talking.

Alexis had his arm around me, and his head leaned back against the seat. I figured he was probably dozing, and I figured that was probably good for him.

I was still relieved, though, when Irena pulled the Audi into a parking spot in Zwickau's main shopping district. She turned around to face us. "What do you need?"

I blinked at her; that caught me off guard. "I can come in with you and--"

"I think it might be best if you wait here," she interrupted. "Have you looked at your clothes?"

Confused, I looked down at myself, and in the low, cold light of the streetlamps, I saw what she meant. My blouse was stained with blood where Alexis had leaned on me.

"Yes, I suppose you are right," I said, looking quickly away. "I need--I don't know, a first aid kit? I have to clean up his wounds. And some painkiller. He has to be hurting."

She nodded, and handed me a notepad and a pen. "Write down your clothing sizes for me, please. I'm afraid neither of you are very presentable, and we will have to go among the public again, before this is over."

I scribbled the information down, and handed back the pad and pen. "Irena, this is going to be expensive. Let me--"

She cut me off with a black look. "Do not speak to me of money. There are bigger things here."

She grabbed her purse and left the car without another word.

I watched her disappear in the sudden silence. What had

that been about? Clearly Irena had a lot at stake here. I just couldn't see what it was.

"Chris," Alexis rasped from beside me. "I'm sorry."

"I thought you were asleep! You should be resting. And what on earth do you have to be sorry for?"

"I should have listened to you. You told me something bad would happen. You told me they would come back."

I sighed. "No, Alexis, I should have listened to you. You wanted to go home, and I convinced you to stay. I'm sorry. I really thought they were only after me, after the thing in the park. I thought we would be able to hold them off until after your performance. I was an idiot. If I had known--if I had *dreamed* they would go after you..."

Alexis squeezed me against him with the arm that was around my shoulders. It must have hurt, but he did it anyway. "Shh," he said. "It's all right. You got me out of there."

"Alexis, what did they want from you?"

He shrugged painfully. "I don't really know. They kept asking me questions--like they asked you--it didn't make any sense. They were waiting in the car when I came out of the menswear shop--they took my cell phone and drove me to a part of town I didn't recognize."

"Was it the Pulverturm?"

"You mean the little tower where you found me? I didn't even know that had a name." He shook his head. "No, this was somewhere else. Not far at all from the shop-- someone's basement, I think. They asked me a lot of questions that didn't make sense--did I know Irena Katarovski, what had she asked me for, had I called my father--crazy, stupid things. But they were serious about it. They would knock me down, kick me, haul me back up by my shirt and shout the question in my face again. But they never believed anything I told them. When they decided they weren't getting the answers they wanted, they said they would move me to where they had more 'tools' to persuade me." He sighed. "But I was telling them the truth."

I didn't trust myself to speak. I sat stone still with my hands clenched, nails digging into my palms, forcing myself to listen. Alexis needed to say this, to get it out of his system. So I had to listen.

"They wanted to move me, but we were still in or close to the shopping district where we might be seen, and my clothes were ruined and a bit blood-stained. They made me change into the tuxedo I had picked up, and one of them burned my old clothes. That worried me."

I nodded. That didn't sound good--disposal of evidence? It sounded like those two had planned to kill Alexis from the moment they grabbed him.

I shivered.

"Me too," Alexis said, kissing the top of my head. "Do you want me to stop?"

"No. No, go on--I need to know what happened to you."

"After we got to the tower, things got really bad," he said, as if what he had already described wasn't bad enough. "They seemed to honestly believe that I knew something I wasn't telling them. They had pipes and things they hit me with, they had these long matches they would put between my toes and light, then just let them burn down. They shot me up with stuff--I don't know what it was, but it must have been hallucinogenic. They threatened you--my God, Chrispen, they threatened you with horrible things, foul, obscene, unspeakable things." He closed his eyes, and shook his head. "I would have told them, if I'd had answers. I would have told them anything, sold out anyone. They didn't believe me."

A silence fell over the car, heavy and oppressive. I clenched and unclenched my fists, trying my best to come to terms with what I had just learned. I didn't see how he was coherent, how he was even conscious. I had never felt such anger, such hate, such pure, livid fury as I did right then.

"Chrispen?" Alexis sounded tentative. "Are you okay?"

"Am I okay?" I sounded choked. "Am *I* okay? How can you even ask me that, with the shape you are in, with the things that just happened to you? The last thing you should be worrying about is me!"

"Calm down."

"I don't know if I can. Listen, Alexis, I am glad I shot that man. Do you hear me? Glad!"

"Chrispen--"

"Wait. Have you thought that through? I killed a man. I broke the law, I broke one of the ten commandments. And if that man showed up tomorrow, I would do it again. Are you okay with that? People have called you a monster, but the real monster is the one you're married to!"

"Such energy," Alexis sighed. "I wish I had that energy right now. But I don't, so I'm going to have to ask you to stop interrupting me and listen. You are no monster, Chrispen. There is a difference between killing to defend yourself and killing for--for whatever reason they thought they had. And if you had given me the gun, I would have done the same thing."

"Really?"

"Really. So if you are a monster, so am I."

"We can be monsters together."

Alexis laughed, but he sounded unutterably tired. "I suppose we can. But I want you to remember something. You can't put yourself in the same category as those men, Chrispen. They weren't killing to defend themselves or anyone they cared about. They killed because it was their job, and they were good at it, and they enjoyed it. That's so different from what you did, I don't even have words for it."

I didn't have a response for that. I just sat, letting it sink in.

"Can I ask you something?" Alexis sounded hesitant.

"Hmm?"

"How did you find me?"

"Irena. She knew where you were, and she got us in."

"Hmm. That seems odd."

I couldn't argue. "There's a whole lot about this situation that's odd. I haven't figured her out yet, but I'm not pushing too hard, to be honest. I would never have gotten you back without her help."

As if on cue, we saw Irena approaching, loaded down with shopping bags. I had no idea how she had managed to buy so much in so short a time.

"Here we go," she said, piling shopping bags into the backseat next to me. "I think you will find everything you will need in these bags." She leaned into the car and held out a drink carrier with four tall, covered, styrofoam cups.

"Coffee?"

"Coffee?" I said in some surprise. "This late?"

Irena shrugged apologetically. "I am afraid there will not be sleeping tonight, at least not for me. We have at least six hours of driving ahead of us."

"Six hours," Alexis echoed, and he reached out and took a cup. I followed his lead--I had eaten exactly nothing all day, and even plain coffee sounded good--anything to keep my stomach from being completely empty. "Where are we going?"

Irena took the remaining two cups and disappeared around to the front of the car, putting the cups into the cupholder and buckling in. "Zurich," she said.

I choked on my coffee. The coffee was pretty hot-- choking on it was not pleasant. "No *way*. Zurich, Switzerland? Tonight? Are you serious?"

She smiled at me in the rear-view mirror. "I am. We have a friend to meet there. Now drink your coffee--we will have a lot of things to talk about, and I need you both to be awake."

What could we do? We shut up and drank our coffee, as the Audi rolled smoothly out of Zwickau and into the black, still night.

♫

I waited for Alexis to finish his coffee--he looked like he needed it--before I did anything else. But as soon as he set his cup aside, I was digging through the bags Irena had brought back. A couple of bags were full of clothes, so I just set them aside. The rest, though--Irena had bought much more than I had thought to ask for.

I fished out a cotton cloth and a bottle of hydrogen peroxide, and went to work carefully removing ruined bits of tuxedo and swabbing at what was left. He was such a mess it was difficult to tell at first where he was actually hurt.

"That's cold," Alexis complained, "and I don't think I like it."

"Hush now," I said. "We've got to get you cleaned up."

I sucked my breath between my teeth--once the tattered remains of his dress shirt were out of the way a series of long, narrow gashes stood angry and red against his chest. "Good Lord, Alexis--what did this to you?"

He winced. "The whip, I think."

"I must apologize." Irena spoke very quietly from the front seat. "That was a trap, but it was not meant for you."

"Not for us?" I echoed, confused. "But they took Alexis!"

Irena shook her head. She seemed sad. "I'm afraid your husband was only the bait. The trap was intended for me."

"For...you?" Belatedly the light bulb came on, and I understood suddenly why Suit Number One had let me go in Schwanenteich. Irena had been his true target all along. I could feel my brain grinding reluctantly into gear. "So...it wasn't you who trashed our hotel room--it was the suits. And you weren't trying to threaten us...you were trying to warn us?"

Irena nodded. "They were desperate to stop me from contacting you. When they found that I already had...they would have done anything to find out what I had told you, to stop it from spreading."

"Spreading," Alexis repeated. I was grateful for the

conversation to distract him; it had made it much easier to finish cleaning those gashes, and now I needed to figure out how to bandage them. "What exactly did they think you had told us?"

That was the question, wasn't it? It seemed to me that this whole conversation had been working up to the answer. And yet, now that it came down to it, Irena seemed to have cold feet. She glanced at Alexis in the rear-view mirror, then resolutely back at the road, her lips set in a thin, tight line.

Alexis looked at me in evident confusion; it seemed he didn't understand this sudden change any more than I did. I looked at Irena's white-knuckled death grip on the steering wheel and tried to think it through.

Alexis had been taken expressly because the suits knew she would come to rescue him. What could be so important that she would risk her life for the chance to tell us--only to chicken out when the moment arrived?

Things fell into place with a click that seemed audible, and I suddenly understood. She wasn't afraid of Alexis or the suits--what Irena feared now was his reaction--his rejection.

"You're not really Irena Katarovski, are you?" I finally said.

She looked at me almost gratefully in the rearview mirror. "No. That is to say, the world does know me by that name, yes. But it is not really mine."

"Not really yours?" Alexis said. "I don't understand. If that isn't your real name, then what is?"

Irena bit her lip and looked away.

"Irena," I said, "forgive me...but is your real name

Natalya Bruskalov?"

The gasp that came from Alexis at those words far surpassed any sound he had made while I swabbed out his wounds. If I was wrong, the mistake I'd made was incalculably huge. But I couldn't forget those eyes, just like Alexis's eyes, eyes that were identical to his father's.

A single tear tracked down Irena's pale face. "Yes," she said, and the sound was little more than a whisper. "I am Natalya Bruskalov."

"Wait...but...how..." Alexis spluttered. He couldn't seem to get a coherent word out. "You disappeared thirty years ago--when my father was accused of treason. His whole family was destroyed. I--I thought you were dead!"

Irena--Natalya?--smiled sadly. "Why wouldn't you? It is what usually would have happened. My story, however, is not usual."

"Will you tell us?" Alexis sounded more alert than he had at any time since we brought him out of the tower.

Natalya frowned. "You do need your rest. But I suppose that is an impossibility now. Very well. I will tell you what I can. Make yourself comfortable, because this is not a short tale."

CADENZA
Natalya's Story

I must tell you first of all that I was not aware of anything strange as I grew up. My mother, Anya Katarovski, was affectionate but often sad. My father was distanced from me and very stern. But these are only my impressions looking back; at the time I thought of them merely as my parents, and nothing more.

At times some random occurrence would trigger a sort of phantom memory. These memories never fit in with my life as I knew it; they always involved a man younger, and handsomer, and happier than my father, and a beautiful blonde woman. I did not know those people, and I did not know what to make of these false memories. They did not make sense, and so I discarded them.

I discovered when I was young that I had a natural propensity for the violin. I wanted nothing more out of life than to play it--constantly. But in this one thing my parents opposed me as in no other. I was forbidden to own a violin, to touch a violin, and all of my attendants were threatened with immediate termination should they allow me access to one. My history tutor once timidly suggested to my father that it was a shame to suppress such talent; he felt I could be great. I never saw him again.

After some monstrous screaming rows, my father finally agreed to allow me to play--but only if I played the viola. He was absolutely adamant that I must never play the violin. My mother disagreed. She felt that it was a mistake to allow me to play anything with strings. I never understood their attitude toward music, but it continued throughout my life.

When I was seventeen I joined the Maestri Soviet. This, as you may imagine, was the subject of our most heated arguments yet--my father flatly forbade me to join any professional touring orchestra. It wasn't until they caught me in the act of running away that he acquiesced--but with some of the strangest conditions imaginable. I would not be permitted to sit first chair. I would not be featured in any solo performances--with the Maestri or anyone else. I would never be permitted to move to violin. I would give no interviews, make no appearances, even backstage. They made me agree to these conditions. The executive director of the Maestri Soviet had to sign a contract binding them to these conditions.

And yet, even with those bizarre conditions, it did not seem as though my family wanted to hide my association with the Maestri. It seemed that they only wanted to hide that I was any good. Much was made of my career as a touring musician, my status as an "emissary to the West", which was laughable--but they always seemed to imply that a mid-section chair in the viola section was the best I could do.

I had been with the Maestri Soviet about a year when we performed in Paris for the first time since I had joined. It was late at night on our first day there, and we were all headed back to our rooms after an exhausting rehearsal that had run long, when Dmitri Kast called me over and asked me to stop in the hotel lounge for a drink with him.

Dmitri Kast! Our concertmaster, and the finest violinist I had ever known. How could I say no? I walked to the lounge with him, making small talk about our rehearsal, the program, and the venue.

Dmitri found us a quiet table in a back corner of the room, and asked for two bottles of wine, two glasses, and the rest of the night undisturbed.

"What are we drinking to?" I asked him, holding a glass of strong red wine and eyeing those two bottles with some trepidation. What reason could he have to think we needed so much to drink?

"Tonight we drink to friends," he said solemnly. "To new friends, and to old friends perhaps discovered again."

"Which one am I?" I was being deliberately facetious, hoping to lighten the mood.

Unfortunately, Dmitri seemed entirely oblivious to my

feeble attempt. "A little of both, I think." The serious way he looked at me made me uncomfortable, and I drank deeply of my wine to cover it.

Dmitri refused to speak again until I had emptied the first glass and started on a second. The bartender elbowed the waiter and said something, jerking his head in our direction. They laughed crudely, but the tension at our little table had nothing to do with sex. I knew very well Dmitri wished the wine to lower my resistance, but not to his advances. The bartender saw an older man wooing a woman young enough to be his daughter, but I could see this was much more serious than that.

How can I possibly convey to you the life-changing conversation I had with Dmitri Kast that night? Dmitri had a network of contacts--spies, some might call them--and he had been watching the Katarovski family since well before I was born. He told me of this. He told me of his best friend, the famous virtuoso and infamous traitor, Alexei Bruskalov, father of the superstar Alexis Brooks in his new life in America. Dmitri had not seen him for fifteen years, for everyone's protection. He told me of the disappearance of Natalya Bruskalov. And he told me the truth about the man I knew as my father.

Petrov Katarovski, as you may know, is a great-grandson of Joseph Stalin. He has always seen that as a great honor--I can assure you I was not raised with the same view of Stalin as you possess, or even the average Russian possesses. My father spoke often of my sacred duty--every Katarovski's sacred duty--to continue the family line, and always to work for a return to Stalin's ideals. It might not surprise you to learn that many have questioned Petrov Katarovski's sanity, but none too loudly, as the Katarovski family is highly placed in many facets of government, and a prime donor to many others. Petrov holds the strings to many highly placed puppets.

And yet, despite the clear imperative of his sacred duty, Petrov and Anya faced many difficulties in attempting to have children. After many miscarriages and several stillbirths, Anya finally delivered a frail, pale baby they called Irena. Irena was a sickly girl, and spent much of her early childhood in various states of illness. When she was three years old, Irena contracted a serious case of pneumonia. She had private doctors and the best care they could provide, but despite all of their efforts, the child died.

Insane in his grief, Petrov declared that the Katarovski family could not die. Irena's birth had left Anya unable to conceive again, but there was another, more ghastly option open to him, and he did not hesitate to take it. Any sane person would have shied away, but Petrov ordered a raid on manufactured charges against the first family he thought of who had a daughter of the right age, similar in size and physical appearance--Alexei Bruskalov, who had been featured on a state-sponsored news program a couple of weeks before. Alexei himself escaped the net Petrov's puppets cast, but Aleksandr Bruskalov--Alexei's father--was tortured to death, and Alexei's wife Elena died soon after in a forced labor camp for the families of traitors.

But three year old Natalya, with her pale complexion, blonde hair, and fragile build--little Natalya disappeared from history. Through his network of contacts, Dmitri had learned that Natalya had been taken through a series of safehouses. A different person brought her to each safehouse, and then was never seen alive again. Two days after the Bruskalov raid--two days after Irena Katarovski left forever this mortal sphere--Natalya Bruskalov was brought quietly onto the Katarovski Estate in the dead of the night, installed in Irena's room, and the long, slow process of reprogramming began.

It was 2 a.m. when we left the bar, followed by the loud guffaw of the bartender, who thought he saw a drunken young woman hanging all over Dmitri Kast. It is true that I had trouble walking without assistance, but that had nothing to do with wine, or with Dmitri himself. My world had just been turned completely upside-down. I didn't even know who I was. The person I had believed myself to be had been dead for many years, buried in an unmarked grave in the courtyard of the Katarovski Estate. The person Dmitri had told me I was didn't exist for me--just an unfamiliar name, attached to other unfamiliar names. I couldn't imagine how I would ever feel normal again.

In the bright light of the next morning, though, I found it all hard to accept. The human mind is resistant to sudden changes in the fabric of life--at least mine was. Dmitri's story had been convincing, but what real reason did I have to believe him? Perhaps I had been a victim of a practical joke--something like an initiation.

Only every time Dmitri looked at me, there was that same genuine sadness in his eyes. I did some research on his alleged best friend, Alexei Bruskalov, and found that everything he had told me was true, including the sudden disappearance of his three-year-old daughter. Alexei had been with the Maestri in Paris when the raid occurred, as Dmitri had said--in fact he had been staying at that same hotel, which struck me as creepy.

Alexei Bruskalov had toured with the Maestri Soviet for quite a few years. We still had members who remembered him well, including a cellist who had become something of a surrogate father to me within the group. I worked up my courage and finally asked him one day about Alexei.

His eyes went misty, and he spoke fondly and at length about the man our country regarded as a traitor. Nothing he told me could be easily reconciled with official reports of the man's betrayal.

When he was finished, he turned to me. "You have his eyes," he said softly, and refused to speak any further on the subject.

I stood later in front of the mirror in my hotel room, a publicity photo of Alexei Bruskalov held up next to my own face. Our coloring was different, the shapes of our faces only similar, but our eyes--there was no denying it, our eyes were *identical*.

Except for the tears in mine.

At that point I did what was, in retrospect, a very unwise thing. I did not stop to consult Dmitri, or my cellist friend, who could have warned me. I left my hotel room in the middle of the night with my viola and a suitcase, and caught a taxi to the airport. I was on the very next plane back to Russia, to confront these people who had stolen my family, my entire life. I think some part of me still refused to believe this thing was true, until I had heard it from them.

You can imagine how well that conversation went. They demanded to know where I had heard--fortunately I had the sense not to tell them that. Until that moment, I'd had no idea the man I had called father could be so cold, so cruel. Now, I got to see him as many others had before and have since, and it was an experience I have never forgotten.

Petrov freely admitted the truth of every charge I laid against him. Alexei Bruskalov had never betrayed his country--neither he nor any member of his family had in any way deserved what had happened to them. None of that mattered, he said, all of that was as nothing next to the responsibility of keeping the Katarovski line alive, even if only in name.

A responsibility which he now laid squarely on me. We both knew the truth of my parentage, but Petrov made it his mission that I should live out the rest of my life under the pretense of his. From that day forward, the Maestri Soviet became my prison. It was put out to the media and the public that my flight back to Russia had been in fear; fleeing from an anonymous stalker and threats that had been laid against my life. Petrov made a lot of convincing noise about the safety of his daughter being his paramount concern, and Katarovski agents--officially something like bodyguards--accompanied our tours from then on. You saw two of them today. They are not easy to evade. They screened my mail, they monitored my phone calls. I don't know what my father told the executive director, but a Maestri Soviet tour never goes anywhere near any member of the Bruskalov family.

Last year I finally accepted that I could not subvert these obstacles. I went late one night to Dmitri's room--rumors about a romance between us have existed ever since that night in Paris, and we find them useful alibis as I help him with his undercover work--and vented my frustration. He offered to go make contact for me; his name was clean, no one would suspect if a solo appearance was scheduled. And so he arranged to guest with the Newton Philharmonic Symphony Orchestra. But before he could make the appearance, he was intercepted and beaten by Katarovski bodyguards. He was hospitalized, and the story was put out that he had pneumonia. I sat at his bedside and cried heavy tears that burned with guilt. This had befallen him because he had taken a chance attempting to help me. I vowed to continue trying to reach my family, but to allow no other person to be at risk while I did so.

This week, the Maestri Soviet performed in Bonn, the day before you arrived in Zwickau. Dmitri and I couldn't imagine how that had been allowed; it must have been a dreadful oversight. Perhaps they did not imagine you would begin rehearsals for your engagement so early. But we could not squander the opportunity. Immediately after the performance, Dmitri went south to Zurich. I sneaked out of my hotel room window to evade the agents and went east to Zwickau.

Of course, they knew immediately upon finding the empty room the next morning where I had gone. And I found to my horror that I had broken my vow--both of you were in danger as soon as I entered Zwickau. I couldn't even warn you; they somehow jammed the signal from my cell phone, and by the time I got around that problem, you already thought I was working with them. I would have turned around and gone back to the Maestri immediately if it would have spared you, but I fear that would only have increased your danger. Feel free to hate me for everything that has happened to you, I won't blame you. I ask but one thing: that you remember I was only trying to reclaim my family, a family who doesn't know that I even exist.

MOVEMENT TWO:
Flight to the West

There was a long silence in the car after Natalya finished speaking, while we tried to process everything she had just told us. Her story brushed up against mine in ways I hadn't expected--I remembered when Dmitri Kast canceled his performance with us due to pneumonia. I certainly hadn't expected anything sinister about it; no one had. Of course I had heard the rumors about Dmitri's clandestine affair with a woman over twenty years his junior, but I always just assumed he was a womanizer. It's unfortunately common among concert violinists, though obviously not universal.

"No one here hates you, Natalya," Alexis said slowly. "At least, I can assure you that I don't, and if I know Chrispen, your story just dissolved any hard feelings she may have harbored as well. And my father--our father--has never forgotten you. He still believes you will find him in America one day."

"If only he could know how I've tried." Natalya had tears in her eyes.

"Well, you will be able to tell him yourself," Alexis said, "assuming we all make it out of here alive."

I shivered; that sounded particularly ominous to me. Alexis squeezed my shoulders, trying to comfort me. It helped, but only a little.

Because I knew he was right.

♫

Natalya had every intention of driving all the way to Zurich herself. It seemed too much to me--with the Katarovski suits after her, who knew when she had last slept properly? A six hour drive in the dark was pushing too far.

I finally convinced her of this as well, and along the side of a foreign highway, we all changed seats. I took the driver's seat and Alexis rode shotgun. Natalya climbed into the backseat. She looked utterly spent, and she seemed to be asleep before I even buckled in.

"Nice of you," Alexis said, "to offer to help drive."

"Do you think so? Maybe it's just a ruse. Maybe I'm headed to the authorities right now to turn her in."

He scooted around in his seat until he was turned sort of facing me. "So you think she made that story up? She isn't my sister at all?"

I shook my head, laughing softly. "Nah, I'm just messing with you. She's your sister, I've no doubt of it. She isn't kidding about her eyes, they hit me the first time I saw her without those sunglasses."

"Well, that's a relief. I thought maybe I was just being gullible, believing her so easily."

"No. I don't doubt her story. That Petrov Katarovski is a real piece of work, but we already knew that. The American Embassy pretty much spelled it out for me."

"The American Embassy?" Alexis sounded surprised. "You went there?"

I nodded. "Wilhelm Braun drove me there. I didn't have anywhere else to go."

"What did they say?"

My fingers clenched tighter around the steering wheel--I could see my knuckles turn suddenly white by the light of the dashboard instruments. "He spent quite a bit of time trying to convince me you left on your own."

"What?"

"Evidently lugging a wife around was getting in the way of all your fans trying to throw themselves into your bed. That was his helpful analysis, anyway."

"What a lot of tommyrot." Alexis actually sounded angry. "I'm sorry you had to go through that. Didn't he have anything helpful to say at all?"

"His attitude did change when I brought the Katarovski name into the conversation. I don't know whether he thought you were voluntarily involved with them or not, but at that point he got me a ride to the airport and plane tickets home."

"I didn't think the embassy did that."

"They don't. It was a personal favor, because my situation was so bad." I shrugged. "It's hard to hold a grudge against someone who goes so far above and beyond to help you. So I guess I have to forgive him for his assumptions about you."

"Oh, dear," Alexis said. He reached over and patted my leg. "You don't need to worry about my sullied honor. Fame is always more glamorous when viewed from the outside."

"I know." It would have been a good moment for a mood-lightening joke, but I remembered seeing my own underwear on the evening news and didn't have the heart to make it.

"I only have one more question," Alexis said, and he sounded hesitant. "Should we call my father?"

I blinked. I hadn't even thought of that. On the surface, it seemed like a given; Alexei had waited more than half his life for this news. But then again...

"You're going to think I'm completely heartless," I said, "but I don't think that would necessarily be a good idea. I think if we tell him now, we may actually be putting him in danger."

"Hmm." Alexis seemed to be considering what I'd said, but I had the impression he'd thought this all through before he brought it up. "I think you're right. That is precisely what those two kept asking me--if I knew who she was and whether I had told my father. What if I had said yes?"

"Exactly. The sad thing is, we don't have to actually tell him anything to put him in danger--they just have to decide that we did. I don't think we can lessen his risk by not calling him, but we would definitely raise it if we did."

Alexis nodded and relaxed into his seat, wincing. He seemed to feel better just knowing we were on the same page.

I pulled the Audi into the next fuel station we came to. I

stopped next to a pump, shut off the engine, and noticed Alexis unbuckling his seat belt.

"What are you doing?"

He looked surprised. "Getting out to pump gas."

"Are you crazy?" I demanded. "Look at you! You're in no shape to do anything but sit right there in that seat. Good grief, I'm a grown woman, I can pump my own gas."

"Chivalry is dead," he sighed.

"It is tonight. I'll tell you what, next time I'm beaten half to death by a couple of thugs, you can take care of the gas."

"Deal," he said, and sank back into the seat. Even with the coffee and the painkillers, I didn't see what was keeping him going.

"Why don't you try to get some sleep?" I suggested, unbuckling my seat belt and pushing open the door.

He yawned, but shook his head. "I'll sleep when you do."

I kissed him and got out of the car. What could I say? Stubborn, stubborn, sweet Alexis. What would I do without him?

Standing under the harsh lights of a foreign gas station, I shivered. I had come all too close to finding out.

I focused on the sounds of the running pump, trying to drown out my own thoughts. I couldn't see where we were going; I couldn't imagine how this would all end. Against the odds, Natalya had broken through; she'd made contact and we knew the truth.

So what? We were running now, and where did that end? In Zurich? I couldn't believe that. These people were persistent, and they were desperate. I couldn't see any way to stop them. Would we be running for the rest of our lives?

It seemed to me the rest of our lives might prove to be rather short.

♪

Before we left the gas station, we all ducked into their restrooms to change into some of the clothes Natalya had bought us. It was a relief. A clean set of clothes, a freshly washed face, and a handful of water through my hair may not have made me a whole new person, but I felt like at least half of one.

We switched drivers one more time that night. This time it was Alexis and I who fell asleep before the car even started moving.

I woke up when Natalya put the car in park and cut the engine. Dawn was just breaking, casting a thin light over our surroundings that was not sufficient to turn off the automatic streetlamps.

We were in a parking lot, in front of a large, modern-looking complex of condominiums.

Natalya turned around to face us. "This is it. Everyone out."

"Alexis." I shook his arm; he was sleeping so heavily he didn't even seem to notice. "Alexis, honey, we're here. You have to wake up."

Natalya opened the door next to him, but it didn't bother him at all. If he had been leaning on it, he'd had fallen right out on the pavement, but he didn't wake up, or even stir.

"I don't like this," I said fretfully. "He shouldn't be this hard to wake. Do you think he's all right?"

"I'm sure he is." Natalya leaned in and slapped each of his cheeks in turn. "Considering what he has been through, sleep is probably the best thing for him. Unfortunately, we do not have the time right now."

Her stinging slaps finally roused him. He turned his head, trying to get away. "Chrispen?"

"She's right here." Natalya's tone was soothing, but she grabbed his arm and hauled him out of the car. "You're both safe. And I intend to keep you that way. But we have to get inside."

I slid out of the car behind Alexis and took his other arm, prepared to help support him wherever we needed to go. It turned out to be unnecessary; the cool morning air seemed to have a good effect on him.

I couldn't help looking over my shoulder as we headed up the walk. I noticed Natalya was doing the same thing. I wasn't sure if that made me feel better or worse.

We all huddled under the little eave like we were trying to hide, while Natalya knocked on the door.

A man's voice spoke at the door, just loud enough for us to hear. "How many roads must a man walk down?"

Natalya rolled her eyes. "Forty-two. Dmitri, that is the worst secret question ever. Bad guys read Douglas Adams too, you know."

"Not in my world, they don't." We could hear him fumbling with the latch, and a moment later the door swung open. The craggy, rugged face of Dmitri Kast, familiar from so many photos and album covers, beamed down at us. "Ah, Irena. It is good to see you safe." He stepped back to let us inside.

"Call me Natalya." She walked past him into the condo's living room.

"So she has told you already? Very good. I am Dmitri Kast."

"I know that." Alexis sounded like he might be suppressing a laugh. He held out his hand for a handshake. "I'm Alexis Brooks."

Dmitri did laugh out loud; a big, boisterous laugh that put us right at ease. "As if there is any way I could not know that!" He pumped Alexis's hand enthusiastically. "It is an honor to finally meet such an extraordinary talent."

"I could say the same thing," Alexis said mildly. "My father speaks very highly of you."

Dmitri's smile turned sad. "Ah, yes, your father. A great man, truly great. Please, come in, sit down. You must have many questions for me."

Alexis clapped the older man on the shoulder and walked on in. I started to follow him.

"Don't think I have somehow forgotten you, Mrs. Brooks," Dmitri said, looking at me seriously. "I was hoping I might have an opportunity to thank you personally."

"Thank me? What on earth for?"

He smiled gently. "Natalya may have mentioned that I have many ways of staying informed. I have seen how much you have done for Alexis, and for Natalya."

"Natalya?" I was beginning to feel a bit like an echo, but this name surprised me. "Have I helped her?"

"More than you know." He scanned the parking lot with a quick glance, and leaned against the door frame. "Do you realize, for instance, that if Natalya had gone to the second floor of the Pulverturm, with or without you, she would have been lost?"

"No. I hadn't realized that. I only made her stay because it seemed best if they didn't know everything we had. She was our ace in the hole, so to speak."

"Indeed. It was a good instinct. If she had gone up there they would have recaptured her and returned her to Russia, and you and Alexis would both have been killed."

I swallowed hard; that was one suspicion I did not like having confirmed. "They would really have killed us?"

"Oh, yes. They would not have taken Alexis otherwise. It would not do to underestimate Petrov Katarovski as an enemy. You were very clever."

I shook my head. "I was very dumb and very lucky."

Dmitri patted my shoulder. "You mustn't be too hard on yourself. None of us could have done better against such opponents. You should not regret killing one of these men-- or more, if it should come to that."

I nodded. That much we could agree on--they had come far too close to killing Alexis, even with our intervention. I would never regret pulling that trigger. I wondered what sort of person that made me.

"Come inside." Dmitri stood back and waved me past. "We have much to discuss."

I walked into the condominium's sunken living room, my head spinning. Here was I, just a couple of years out of Juilliard, married to an international icon, and rubbing elbows with another like we were old friends. And apparently, all of us were now involved in some sort of international intrigue.

And my husband's half-sister, gone for thirty years, had just come back from the dead, very much alive and up to her eyeballs in our current problems.

It was a lot to take in.

The condo had white carpet, and white leather furniture. Natalya was settled into an overstuffed chair with her eyes closed, looking as though she could collapse. Alexis sat on the couch, leaning his head back, looking much the same as Natalya. I might have expected the gleaming white upholstery to have put some color into his face by comparison. I would have been wrong. He looked as pale and wan as before, which I found, frankly, alarming. I sat down beside him gingerly, trying not to disturb him.

Alexis put his arm around me without opening his eyes.

"You look like you've had a rough night," Dmitri said, taking a seat across from Natalya.

Natalya cracked an eye at him.

"You could say that," Alexis said. "This is a nice place, Dmitri. Yours?"

"Sadly, no." Dmitri looked around the room as though he was just now seeing it. "It belongs to an associate of mine. She has relocated for the moment, and kindly agreed to let us meet here."

Alexis nodded, as if that was pretty much as he had expected. Exhausted as he was, he was probably way beyond much surprise anyway.

"I do apologize," Dmitri sighed. "Things were not supposed to go like this. Natalya and I truly believed we could protect you. Obviously we underestimated how desperate they are, how far they are willing to go to keep this secret."

"Obviously," Natalya said dryly.

Dmitri cocked an eyebrow at her, then looked us all over carefully. "I am sorry there is no time for sleep. Clearly that is what is needed here, more than anything else. Sadly, though, we are not--as you Americans say--out of the woods yet. We must keep moving, if we are to succeed."

"Keep moving where?" Alexis sounded unutterably tired. "Zurich wasn't on my agenda to begin with."

"Please bear with me but one more moment, and we shall discuss precisely that." Dmitri disappeared into the condominium's small kitchen.

It was quiet and still, and we were comfortably ensconced in cozy furniture. I think all of us could easily have fallen asleep--napping in the car had kept us conscious, but none of us were what you would call rested. I didn't see how Alexis was still staying upright.

Dmitri was back before we had time to miss him, carrying a big tray loaded with coffee mugs, fruit pastries, bagels with cream cheese, and a large, thick plastic folder. He placed the tray on the coffee table, and tossed the folder into his chair. "Please, eat. I know you must all be hungry."

In truth we were, but I think any of us would have taken a short nap over a king's feast right then. I know I would have.

But a nap wasn't an option, and food was right in front of us, so we each settled in with a cup of coffee and our choice of breakfast foods and tried to make the best meal of it we could under the circumstances.

"Where are your violins?" Dmitri asked. It was pretty much the last thing I had expected him to say.

"At the hotel in Zwickau," I said around a bite of cherry

danish. "I called and had them held there until we could pick them up."

"This is good," Dmitri said. "The two of you, with your violins--everyone in the world would know who you are."

Natalya frowned. "Are we hiding from everyone in the world now?"

Dmitri nodded. "I am afraid so. Things have changed since you left Zwickau."

"We're being followed?" I said fretfully.

"Well, yes," Dmitri said, "but we expected that. What I did not expect was the media exposure Katarovski has given to the situation."

"Media exposure?" Natalya sat up straighter. "I did not think that Petrov Katarovski would willingly involve the media in this."

"He has," Dmitri said, "but on his own terms, as always. The story they are telling is that infamous murderer Alexis Brooks, son of traitor Alexei Bruskalov, has kidnapped Irena Katarovski, pride of the great Katarovski family."

"And people believe that?" My voice burned with indignation.

"People believe what suits them," Dmitri returned gently. "They believed I had pneumonia, did they not? They believed our dear Alexis murdered his first wife. A person might be quite intelligent, Mrs. Brooks, but a mass of people is invariably stupid. They are ready to believe any gossip handed to them, and the dirtier it is, the quicker they will believe it."

"That's pretty pessimistic," I said, but I couldn't really argue it. Since meeting Alexis, I had seen Dmitri's point proven only too many times. "What are we going to do?"

"The only thing we can do." Dmitri pulled the plastic expanding folder onto his lap and opened it. "We are going to get you back to America--you will have the best chance of escape there, if it is possible anywhere. But we can't have you flying as Mr. and Mrs. Alexis Brooks. With those names on your tickets, anyone would recognize you, not just the people who would know you on sight anyway."

"So we are traveling under assumed identities." Alexis still sounded pretty tired, but he was sitting up with his eyes open, which was a definite improvement.

Dmitri grinned. "That's right, Alexis. Or perhaps I should call you Reginald." He pulled out a manilla folder from the expanding file and handed it to Alexis.

Alexis flipped open the manilla folder, and wrinkled his nose. "Reginald Grant, music critic from New York City. I suppose I can live with the critic part--but does it have to be Reginald?"

Dmitri's grin never faltered. "Beggars can't be choosers. The papers are already complete. Besides, it sounds very much like a critic, don't you think?"

"I suppose so. But don't expect a nice review of your next performance."

Dmitri chuckled. He withdrew another folder from the expanding file and passed it across to Natalya. "And you, *dorogaya*, you will be Nadja Rodenof, a postal clerk from Moscow."

"Moscow." She scowled at her folder. "I should be an American. I will have to be, when this is all over."

"Mmm. Certainly it would be possible--if it is also

possible for you to conceal your accent."

Natalya gave him a black look.

"That is as I thought. Let's not ask for trouble, shall we? A woman with a Russian accent claiming to be an American could arouse suspicion." This time, Dmitri handed a folder to me. "And here is your, Mrs. Brooks."

The folder felt heavier than I expected. I spread it open on my lap, and found a short cover sheet with a summary of my new identity--I was traveling as Alannys Gale, a music teacher. A Connecticut driver's license slipped out from behind the cover sheet, with my picture and Alannys's name. There was a passport, a social security card, a birth certificate, and a prodigious stack of American money, held together with a binder clip.

"Well?" Dmitri prompted. "No complaints about your name? Your nationality? Anything?"

I shook my head. "No. This is very thorough--you've been busy. Thank you."

Dmitri held out his hands in my direction. "Finally, someone who appreciates the work I have done. My time in Zurich has not been all relaxation and cherry danishes, I am afraid. There has been much to do. It is well that the Katarovski guards did not move any sooner. If you will look at the back of your folders, you will find money for you to use in America, and plane tickets to get you there."

"This is amazing," I said, flipping through my little packet of tickets. "How can we thank you?"

"No thanks are necessary," Dmitri said, inclining his head. "If we can get all three of you safely back to Alexei, I will be happier than you could know."

"That is the tricky part," Natalya said. "I doubt they will drop their pursuit simply because we arrive in America."

"If we even make it to America," I said grimly.

Everyone looked at me, but nobody seemed to have a response. In the sudden silence we heard a car door slam out front, then another. We all froze, listening intently, looking around at each other in fear.

A hard, loud rap at the front door shattered the quiet.

"This is not good," Dmitri muttered. "How did they find us so quickly?"

Natalya was already on her feet, scanning wildly around the room like she was about to tear her own exit in it.

"Come, *dorogaya*." Dmitri caught her arm just above the elbow and pulled her along with him. "Everyone follow me. Hurry."

We really didn't need to be told. We clutched our folders like talismans and scurried after him, white-faced and silent, gripped with deadly tension.

Dmitri led us through the kitchen and into the dining room, where a large picture window looked out into the courtyard of the condominium complex.

"It's a dead end," Alexis said. He sounded short of breath. I glanced at him sharply, wondering how much more of this he could take.

"It would seem so." Dmitri shoved the drapes back, seeming oblivious to the pounding that was shaking the front door in its frame. If they had used a battering ram, I didn't see how it could have sounded worse. "But appearances are often deceiving."

He flipped a latch on the side of the window frame, and

the whole big assembly swung open. "Go. Get to the airport and get on that plane. I will keep the Katarovski agents here."

Natalya already had one leg out of the window. I looked at Dmitri in sudden fear. "But what about you?"

Dmitri put a hand on my shoulder. "Tell your father-in-law that I did all I could do, for all of you."

He turned and disappeared back through the condo, as quick and silent as a breath of air.

I hesitated, looking after him, unsure what to do. I seemed a very unlikely candidate to play hero. But how could we just leave him?

"Hurry," Natalya urged. "He knows what he is doing. But we have to get out of here before those men get in, or else it will all be for nothing."

I looked at her, torn, and then back into the condo. If Alexis and Natalya went on ahead, surely I could stay and help him...

"It will never work," Natalya said evenly, as though she could read my intent on my face. "Alexis will not leave without you. He can't survive here in his state."

One glance at Alexis affirmed the truth of this. I looked into his tired, haggard eyes and knew that he would die here before he would leave me behind.

I swallowed hard and climbed out of the window. I turned and helped Alexis out, then pushed the big window gently shut.

The latch fell back into place. It was as though we had never been there.

By the time we crept around to the front of the complex,

everything was clear. The door-pounders were gone, presumably inside. I couldn't help but wonder how Dmitri was faring. Did they suspect how deeply he was involved in this, how much he knew?

There was no time for maudlin emotion. Before we even had the back door closed, Natalya was guiding the Audi quickly and quietly out of the parking lot, yanking her seat belt over her shoulder as she drove.

I watched the condominium complex disappear behind us, wondering, would any of us see Dmitri Kast alive again?

From Dmitri's condo to the Zurich Airport was almost an hour's drive.

An hour is a long time to brood over things that may or may not have happened, to glance anxiously at every car that passes, to nervously inspect every vehicle that falls in behind you. But it can be done. Every one of us in that car could attest to that.

The airport was crowded, with streams of people bustling in every direction, and no one was much inclined to pay any particular mind to us, which was a relief. The young man behind the rental counter didn't even glance up when I turned in the car keys; he just announced my total, ran my credit card, and sent me on my way with a half-hearted "good day". He had his nose buried in a book again before I even turned away.

"That was easy," Alexis commented when I joined them where they waited by a pay phone.

"Quite." Natalya's tone was sour; she scanned the crowds around us as though she expected Katarovski suits to jump out of them. Maybe she did. "It is very lucky that boy is too busy with books to pay attention to the news these days."

"True enough." I shifted my weight and pushed my hair behind my ear--she was making me nervous. The way she kept looking around, like a prairie dog scanning hostile plains, did nothing to help me relax in the noisy airport. "What do we do now?"

"We make ourselves a little harder to recognize," she answered, and strode off.

I looked at Alexis, a little taken aback. Alexis shrugged at me and turned to follow her, so I took his arm and went along for the ride, happy just to be with him.

If you've ever shopped in an airport, you know you aren't going to find a completely new you there. We did the best we could--Natalya bought a baseball cap and stuffed her long blonde hair up inside it, and ditched the sunglasses. Alexis bought a pair of big sunglasses in a mirrored style that I didn't even know they made anymore, that hid a lot of his face. And me, I found a pair of square-shaped reading glasses I wore low on my nose, looking at the world over the top of them, and pulled my hair back from my face under a wide headband.

We wouldn't have fooled anyone who actually knew us, but for everyone else, we would be harder to recognize at a glance.

Three people flying halfway around the world with no luggage probably should have seemed odd, but no one seemed to notice or care. Maybe people were too polite, or maybe they were just too busy. We appreciated it either way.

We made it onto the plane and into our assigned seats with no problems, and no sign of the Katarovski agents. It felt like a victory, but as I watched the scenery rush past our plane as it gathered speed for takeoff, I couldn't help but wonder what that victory had cost.

The relative safety of the airplane was comforting. The rumble of the big engines and the white noise hiss of the air put us all to sleep.

Unfortunately the flight from Zurich to Amsterdam only took about an hour and a half. It felt like we had hardly closed our eyes before we were dumped off the plane and into another international airport for a two-hour layover before our flight to Detroit.

"Detroit," I mused, looking at my ticket. "That seems like an odd choice."

Alexis shrugged, looking as uncomfortable as I felt in the hard plastic seats of the boarding gate waiting area. "Probably the first available flight Dmitri found. We're lucky actually--DTW is fairly close to home."

I nodded. "Do you suppose that figured into Dmitri's planning at all--getting us close to home--or was it all just the luck of the draw?"

"Shush," Natalya said from behind us.

I did. It occurred to me that Alexis was supposed to be from New York, and I from Connecticut, and our conversation would seem odd, especially to anyone who might be checking our identification at the boarding gate later. It would be better if we gave them nothing to overhear. Natalya was, as usual, correct.

Two hours is actually pretty reasonable for a layover--goodness knows I've had much worse. And yet, this particular layover felt like it would never end. We were all still pretty tired, but sleep in the airport terminal seemed impossible, and unwise. We had taken our seats in the boarding gate deliberately--Alexis and I facing up the concourse, Natalya facing back down the way we had come.

Alexis moved to put his arm around me, then caught himself and laid it next to mine on the armrest instead. Our assumed identities, we kept reminding ourselves, were not married. "I don't think we'll be seeing those guys here," he said, in his best comforting tone.

Natalya grunted in what might have been agreement. "But vigilance is always wise."

"No argument there," Alexis said, and I understood that he had spoken not for Natalya's benefit, but for mine. I must have been telegraphing my tension to every person in the room.

I shifted in my seat, edging closer to Alexis. "Alex--I mean, Reginald, what makes you so sure we won't see those suits here?"

He chuckled. "Well, we left our concertmaster friend in Zurich what--four and a half hours ago?"

I nodded.

"It's an eight hour drive from Zurich to Amsterdam. Even if they had discovered where we were going right away and set out to follow us, they wouldn't get here before our plane leaves."

"Eight hours if you're following the speed limit," I grumbled. "They could always speed. And what if they fly?

They could be here already." I couldn't help an agitated glance up the concourse.

Alexis shook his head. "I don't think they will. They're armed, remember? I don't think they would be willing to leave their guns, and no one's going to let them on a plane carrying weapons. Even if they drove as fast as their car would go and never got caught, I think they would be cutting it pretty close. And there's still the question of exactly how they would manage to get as far as the boarding gates with their guns."

"Maybe they don't need them," I said darkly.

This time Alexis did put his arm around me, regardless of who might be watching. "I promise you, Chrispen," he said, low and right in my ear, "no unarmed man is going to keep us from getting on that plane."

"Honestly," Natalya said, "why don't you just put up a sign with your names on it?"

We shifted farther away from each other, but Alexis had already achieved his purpose. I felt more at ease than I had since our flight from Zurich. And as I was rapidly learning, any small moment of peace had to be treasured.

Because you never knew when it might be taken away.

"Delta Airlines announces Flight 9524, with service to Detroit, Michigan, final boarding now. Last call for flight 9524 to Detroit."

The voice was pleasant, and heavily accented. The words were difficult to understand and so I didn't, letting them brush up against my awareness and then dissipate again as quickly and with as little notice as they had come.

Dozing in the crowded open airport was a bad idea, I knew that. I seemed to be doing it anyway.

Alexis faked a stretch, managing to poke me in the side as he did. "That's our flight." The words were barely audible, but I heard them clearly.

"Oh, right." I scrambled around for my boarding pass, my papers, and my purse. Natalya was already in the boarding line, and Alexis fell in a couple of places behind her. I gathered my things and got into line a few places behind them. It looked, lucky me, like I would be the last to board.

The line moved quickly. Natalya made it through and disappeared into the boarding ramp without a backward glance. Alexis stood just inside the tunnel, checking his watch, fiddling with his papers, and in general just stalling in every conceivable way. His concern touched me, but how could I possibly get into trouble boarding an airplane?

The gate attendant smiled at me. I smiled back and handed her my boarding pass. Just a few more minutes and I would be safe on the big jet with my husband and sister-in-law, untouchable and headed for the relative safety of my home country.

I don't know what made me look behind me. As the attendant separated my boarding pass from the stub, I reached up to push my new reading glasses a little higher up on my nose. As I did so, I glanced back over my shoulder just in time to see two men in matching dark suits hurrying up the concourse and into the boarding area. They wore their sunglasses indoors, heedless of the unnecessary attention they attracted, which struck me as a bad sign.

Frozen with fear is a common expression, but I'm not sure I ever really understood it until that moment. I couldn't seem to do anything but stare, watching my doom approach as swiftly and silently as sharks in deep water.

"Your pass, ma'am?"

The voice jerked me out of my stupor, calm and polite at my side, completely unaware of the danger.

I tried to smile, accepting my boarding pass stub with hands that were suddenly shaky. She stepped back to let me by, and I risked one last glance behind me.

That's when they saw me. One suit elbowed the other, jerked his chin in my direction, and to my everlasting horror they both started running.

Apparently they no longer cared about drawing unwelcome attention. I found I suddenly didn't care either. I ran into the boarding gate to an obviously startled Alexis, who had not seen what I had seen.

"Suits," I gasped, and I grabbed his arm and we ran headlong down the tunnel towards the plane. We could hear the gate attendant behind us.

"If you gentlemen would care to board, please present your tickets and I'll--*oof*. Hey! You can't--"

The stewardess at the plane's entrance helped us inside, seemingly oblivious to our out-of-breath, rumpled state. We could hear her radio crackle as we hurried to our seats.

"Get that door closed! You've got two men attempting to board without tickets, and they will hurt you to do it."

I forced myself not to look back. I could hear the big door close tight behind us, though, and released a breath I hadn't been aware I was holding. That had been too close.

They had found us with frightening speed. And they knew now which flight we had just boarded.

Whether we liked it or not, they knew where we were headed next.

♫

The Katarovski agents must not have told airport officials who they were chasing or why, because the plane lifted off without further incident. I supposed it made sense--they knew exactly where we would arrive next and when--they had time now to prepare their trap, to meet us on their own terms. I didn't know what happened to the two who stormed the boarding gate in Amsterdam, but it didn't matter. They weren't working alone.

The flight was less that half full. As soon as we hit cruising altitude, all three of us abandoned our assigned seats, which were scattered throughout the cabin, and moved to a row in the back where we could sit together with no one else around.

"What happened?" Natalya whispered, leaning toward me.

I leaned over toward her, and poor Alexis was caught between us. We kept our voices low, and he and I filled her in on what had transpired at the terminal.

She shook her head. "This is bad," she said, as though that wasn't patently obvious. "Very, very bad."

I was inclined to agree, but I didn't really see how stating things that were perfectly plain was going to help us out of our fix. I was in a bad enough mood I might have said so, too, if a slight sound behind me hadn't caught my attention first.

It was our stewardess, standing in the aisle shifting awkwardly from foot to foot. She looked nervous and apologetic, and I suddenly had a bad feeling about this interruption.

"Excuse me," she said, hesitant and shy. Her gaze touched on each of us briefly before coming to rest on Alexis. "I'm sorry to bother you, but--aren't you Alexis Brooks?"

I held my breath, waiting to see what he would say. With so many people hunting us, and so many false accusations against us, it was unquestionably dangerous to acknowledge our identities. And yet, nothing in this lady's demeanor suggested she was out to get us. It's always a bit of a risk to approach someone you think may be famous--and always humiliating if you turn out to be wrong. She had gone out on that limb for Alexis; did he have it in him to just leave her there?

"Yes." The word sounded like a sigh. "Yes, I am."

Natalya glowered like a thundercloud, but the stewardess's face lit up. "Oh, I knew it. I just knew it! I'm sorry to bother you--I could tell you didn't want to be recognized, but I had to come over to say thank you. For my son."

"Your son?" The words were out before I realized I was going to speak. It wasn't my conversation to butt in to, I knew that, but my confusion seemed to have beaten out my manners.

She smiled at me apologetically. "Yes. Kevin Abbott--my son."

Alexis's expression changed instantly. Clearly the name

meant something to him, though it was unfamiliar to me. He seemed stunned. "Then you are..."

"Megan Abbott," the stewardess said. She glanced around self-consciously, but no one else on the plane paid her--or us--any attention, so she turned back and addressed herself to me. "My Kevin was thirteen when he died from leukemia three years ago. But first, he got to spend a day with your husband through the Make A Wish Foundation."

"He was a very talented young man," Alexis recalled.

"He was." Megan brushed a tear from her eye. "That visit with you meant the world to him, Mr. Brooks. He talked about it till the very end. He never forgot it, and neither did I. I can never really repay you for what you did for him, but if there's anything, anything at all, I can ever do for you, I hope you won't hesitate to ask."

"Thank you," Alexis said. He sounded hoarse.

Megan Abbott flashed us all a bright smile and hurried away toward the front of the plane. I watched her go, trying to process what I had just heard.

"I've never heard of a child picking a concert violinist for their wish," I said finally. "That's pretty remarkable."

"He was a pretty remarkable boy." Alexis's smile was sad. "This was only three years after Madeleine's murder, and the entire world still thought I was the monster who did it. But Kevin--he never really seemed to notice all the negative media reports, much less believe them. He wrote me letters after his visit, every week, until..."

I nodded. "And now his mother seems the same way," I remarked. "The manhunt and the kidnapping charges don't seem to have fazed her at all."

"It is a pity everyone is not like her." Natalya's tone had an edge. "It will do us little good to assume new identities if we tell the truth to anyone who asks."

"You're right," Alexis said. "I'm sorry."

But I watched Megan move up the aisle, stopping here and there to answer questions for other passengers. I thought about a boy who chose to spend one of his last days on earth not with a popular athlete, or a famous rock star, but with a concert violinist.

It didn't seem like Alexis had anything to apologize for.

Megan Abbott returned a few hours later with lunch. She handed us cold cut sandwiches on hoagie rolls, bagged potato chips, and cubed fruit bowls. As little as any of us had eaten lately, it looked surprisingly good.

"So," she said, pouring half of a soda into a plastic cup, "you must be Irena Katarovski?" She handed the cup and the can to Natalya.

Natalya froze, then set the drinks stiffly on her tray, with a covert glance around. There was nobody in earshot. "How did you know?"

Megan shrugged. "It's all over the news--the reports that Mr. Brooks kidnapped you. They can't decide whether you," she gestured in my direction with another soda can she was preparing to crack open, "were an accomplice or another victim. There's a lot of speculation."

She poured the soda, then handed the cup and the can to me. I tried to read her face, but it was calm and revealed nothing. "Well," I said, pausing to sip at my soda like this conversation was no big deal, "what do you think?"

"What do *I* think?" Megan laughed. "I think the whole thing is a bunch of hooey!"

I sat back, relieved. "Because you and your son met Alexis before?"

"Well, that certainly helps. But look at you three. Glasses, hats, huddling together here in the back--I'm getting the impression that you are hiding from trouble, not causing it. And just look at Miss Katarovski--she's very comfortable and friendly with you for someone being dragged around against her will."

"There is that." I grinned at Natalya. She smiled back, but hesitantly.

"It's pretty obvious that there's a lot the media isn't telling us. They may even be completely wrong about the whole situation." Megan shrugged. "It wouldn't be the first time."

"No, it wouldn't," Alexis murmured. "Thank you."

"No problem." Megan flashed her bright smile at us again, and pushed her serving cart farther up the aisle.

"She seems nice." Natalya said it like she was still waiting for the sucker-punch behind the smile.

"Yes." Alexis sounded preoccupied. "And she brings up a good point. What are we going to do when we get home? The media is saturated against us."

"The media isn't our only problem," Natalya said grimly. "Petrov Katarovski is not going to give up just because we land inside American borders."

"Then there is only one thing to do," I said, surprising even myself with my confidence. "The only thing capable of pushing back all these lies is the plain truth. The truth is what Katarovski is so desperate to keep hidden. So we are going to have to expose it."

"A press conference," Alexis said, following my line of thought. "As soon as possible after we land. Once the secret is in the open, they will have no more reason to keep fighting, right?"

Natalya nodded, but she looked doubtful. "It will have to be done very quickly, before they catch up with us again."

"As soon as we are allowed to use our cell phones again," Alexis said, "I will call my agent. He can arrange the conference--with all this scandal, we shouldn't have any trouble getting media attention."

Natalya was still nodding. She seemed resigned to the plan--no one had any better ideas, after all.

I was excited. Finally a chance to be proactive in this mess, a chance to strike back at the shadowy hand controlling the pawns. After so much running, it felt good to be doing something--anything--direct that would improve our situation.

And the way things stood, I didn't see how it could get much worse.

♫

It takes almost nine hours to fly from Amsterdam to Detroit. We all got some of the first real sleep we'd had in days, but I think I speak for all of us when I say we were still pretty groggy when the plane began its final descent.

As soon as the rapid deceleration of touchdown was complete, I dug Alexis's cell phone out of my purse. When I pulled it out, I found it already ringing.

The display showed the incoming call was from Alexei

Bruskalov.

I knew the polite thing to do would be to hand the phone to Alexis. Instead I pushed the talk button--I had a feeling this call was not as it appeared, and taking it would not improve my husband's already fragile state. "Hello?"

"Chrispen?" The voice was indeed my father-in-law's, but it was uncharacteristically panicked, almost frantic. Words spilled out so fast that it was difficult to separate them. "Chrispen, *dorogaya,* you must listen to me--whatever these men demand, you must not--"

He abruptly cut off. "Alexei?" I could hear the harsh sounds of the phone being fumbled...a struggle...swearing in Russian. "Alexei, are you there?"

"We have the old man." The voice was cold, utterly emotionless, and unfamiliar, but of course I knew I was dealing with a Katarovski agent. "You have just spoken with him; you know this to be true."

"What do you want?" The words seemed to come from a great distance away. Alexis laid his hand on my arm, but it felt like someone else's arm.

"It is very simple. By now you must know the true name of she who travels with you. You will reveal this to no one. There is a welcoming party of sorts awaiting your plane. Your group will go with this party with no protest. If you speak a word of the truth, Bruskalov will die."

A sharp click disconnected the call.

I lowered the cell phone numbly to my lap, my mind racing frantically, but getting nowhere, finding no way out of the trap they had us in.

"Chrispen?" Alexis already knew something was wrong, I

could hear it in his voice. It sounded off, like everything else around me. "What happened?"

I swallowed hard and shoved the phone back into my purse. "They've got Alexei."

Alexis stared at me, stricken. "No."

I nodded grimly. "They've called out the authorities to meet us when we disembark this plane. We have to go with them, and we can't tell anyone the truth, or they will kill Alexei."

Alexis was a perfect picture of shock. Natalya's hands shook in her lap.

"No," she said fiercely. "It can't end like this. We have come too far to let them win. We must fight this!"

"But how?" I demanded. "They hold all the cards. They know where we're going to land and when we will get there, and they will hear everything we say there. We can't risk Alexei!"

"Is there a problem, folks?" The voice behind me startled me; I had forgotten for the moment that we weren't actually alone. Megan Abbott stood there, regarding us curiously, and it seemed to me, expectantly.

"You could say that," I said slowly. Natalya would disapprove, but Megan already knew so much about our situation, what could it hurt to take her completely into our confidence? "We've just learned we're to be taken into custody when we leave this plane. If that happens, we'll never be able to clear Alexis of this ridiculous charge. But how can we get off of here without being caught?"

"You can't," Megan said, but she sounded thoughtful. "At least, all of you can't. But you, Mrs. Brooks...you're just about my size. I could trade clothes with you."

"What?"

She glanced up the aisle, but no one was paying us any mind. "It is the only way you are getting off of this airplane without going immediately into custody. You can walk out of here as a stewardess. Then one of you will still be free, still be able to fight this."

"But how?" I looked around at my companions, but no one seemed to have any ideas. "Natalya, maybe you should do this."

Natalya bit her lip, and slowly shook her head. "It won't work. My picture has been shown all over the television, the newspapers, the internet--and I cannot conceal my accent."

I sighed, conceding it. I wasn't famous like Alexis, even for the circumstances surrounding me, like Natalya. I was just the girl who married Alexis Brooks, and away from him, I was nondescript enough that no one was liable to know who I was. "You're right. But Megan, I can't ask you to do this. Even if it works, eventually we are going to be found out, and then--"

"I don't care." Megan sounded pretty certain. "Damn the consequences. The only way I can help your husband is by making sure you live to fight another day. And I owe him a debt too big to repay. But I have to try, however I can--it's the only way I have to honor Kevin. He would never forgive me if I didn't help you."

"Thank you." I didn't know what else to say.

Megan grabbed my arm. "We need to hurry. They'll be opening the door soon."

If you've ever been inside an airplane bathroom, you can

probably imagine what it was like for two people to try to change clothes in one. Awkward and uncomfortable, and the less said about it, the better. I gave Megan all of my false documentation.

As soon as we emerged into the aisle, Megan clapped me on the shoulder. "Good luck."

"To you, also," I answered. She grabbed her purse out of a little storage closet and disappeared into the front of the plane, just another passenger eager to de-board.

Alexis and Natalya were waiting for me, quiet and resolved.

"Here." Alexis handed me a thick stack of cash. "This is the money Dmitri gave Natalya and I--I don't think we are going to need it where we're going. Use it any way you need to."

I looked at the money, then stuffed it in my purse with everything else. "They'll be expecting three. What are you going to tell them?"

"We're going to tell them you exited the plane with everyone else. And we're going to tell them we have no idea where you are. Both of those things are true. However you manage to pull us out of the fire, it will be a surprise to us."

I swallowed a sudden lump in my throat, looking away uncomfortably. "I'll do my very best. You know that. But it doesn't look good."

Alexis put his hands on my shoulders and looked at me levelly. "I have complete faith in you."

He did, too. I didn't know whether he was inspired or just completely crazy, but he was telling me the total truth. It didn't do much to take the pressure off, but for some insane reason it made me feel better. I leaned forward and gave him a quick kiss. "I love you," I whispered.

"I love you, too." He stepped back from me, his voice rough. How was I going to do this? I couldn't imagine being away from him again--I had just gotten him back! "You'd better get moving. You'll have a better chance of making it out of here if you leave before us."

I nodded and started briskly down the aisle before any more doubts could set in. I had no idea what waited outside of the plane, but I figured whatever it was, the best way to meet it was head-on.

A kind of blockade had been set up at the end of the boarding ramp. Two or three long, narrow tables had been pushed together, with federal agents sitting behind them checking the disembarking passengers and crew against flight manifests. A few more agents in combat uniforms, conspicuously armed, paced around the area to discourage anyone who might try to interfere with the proceedings, or to circumvent the blockade.

I swallowed hard, my step faltering. I was crazy to think I could bluff my way through this.

I could see Megan standing in front of one of the long tables, talking to an agent who was holding my fake ID.

"Yeah," her voice floated over to me, easy and confident, "I get that a lot. I just went in earlier this week and got my hair bleached and cut short. It's amazing the difference, right?"

The agent looked at her, looked at the ID, and shook his head. "You're telling me," he said, but he handed her back the card and waved her on through.

Another agent, sitting at the end of the line of tables, looked up and saw me standing there and waved me over.

"Name?" he asked as I approached.

I heard the sudden commotion behind me and knew that Alexis and Natalya had come off the boarding ramp. My stomach turned a sudden backflip, but I didn't dare turn around. "Megan Abbott," I said. The noise around us was probably a good thing--it helped hide the way my voice wavered.

"Megan Abbott," the agent repeated. "I have you right here." He checked a name off of the list in front of him, and glanced off to my left. "It looks like they found the ones we're after. You're free to go. Thank you for your time."

I nodded and made my way around the edge of the table. I could hear the sounds of Alexis's arrest behind me; the reading of Miranda rights, agents asking 'Miss Katarovski' if she would mind coming with them to answer a few questions. What I wasn't prepared for was the popping flashbulbs, the rolling television cameras, the reporters with one hand on the microphone and the other over their earpiece, the journalists shouting questions into the fray and scribbling in their steno pads the entire time.

"Miss Katarovski, how does it feel to finally be free?"

"Mr. Brooks, what drove you to commit this terrible crime?"

"Was Chrispen Brooks your accomplice or just another victim?"

"I understand that this is a provisional arrest pursuant to an appeal for immediate extradition from Germany. Can any of the federal agents present comment on the likelihood of that request for expedited extradition being granted?"

"Mr. Brooks, I think everyone here expected your wife to de-board that plane with you--given the speculation, it's frankly disturbing that she isn't here. What can you tell us about the whereabouts of Chrispen Brooks?"

I could tell Alexis had turned to respond to that question by the sudden hush. I could hear his answer clearly across the room.

"I don't know where my wife is at this time. But my heart is with her always."

I hurried down the concourse, blinking back sudden tears.

♫

Extradition. This was what I contemplated on my two-hour taxi ride back to Newton. The taxi driver hadn't been eager to take me on, until I paid him a large wad of Dmitri's cash in advance.

My opinion of the media had sunk pretty low over the years. There was the way they gleefully turned to tear apart their former darling when Alexis had been implicated in Madeleine's murder. They were always there, circling like giant buzzards just out of reach, but ready to descend the moment any hint of trouble surfaced--we had seen that in Zwickau. The stress and unhappiness they caused was very real.

And yet I had a media person of some flavor to thank for this revelation. Germany was pushing for Alexis's extradition. It was the only clue I had to the way things were moving around me, and where they were likely to move next.

Extradition was usually a long and complicated process. The fact that a provisional arrest had already been made-- well, that sure made it seem like someone was putting the rush on this case. I didn't doubt Katarovski had contacts in the German government, but here?

It didn't matter. Things were moving faster than I expected, and I was going to have to move just as fast to keep up.

The first thing I had to do was free Alexis and Natalya to tell the truth. To do that, I was going to have to free Alexei. Once the threat to him was eliminated, the truth could finally come out.

And it had to come out as soon as possible, before Alexis was extradited. I seriously doubted Katarovski had any real intention of letting Alexis stand trial. A trial with Alexis in it would be a high-profile event, and Katarovski wouldn't be able to control what was said on the stand. There would be too big a risk of things coming to light that he did not wish the world to know.

No, I was afraid this extradition was really about getting Alexis out of this country, back to where it had already been demonstrated that Katarovski's men had facilities and influence, back to where he could be made to disappear with much more ease.

And I very much feared that if Alexis disappeared this time, I would never see him again.

So I knew what I had to do, and I knew I had a very limited time to do it. All I had to do now was figure out some way to pull it off.

Sure. Piece of cake.

It was late in the evening when the taxi dropped me off in front of our house in Newton. I gave the driver a few more bills, grateful he had not tried to make small talk with me, and had given me the whole quiet trip to work through my thoughts.

The driver gave me a card with his name and cell phone number on it in case I ever needed another ride.

I turned the key in the front door and let myself in to the home Alexis and I had shared for the last year. Standing there in the dark foyer, surveying the silent rooms and knowing he was in none of them, loneliness washed over me like a physical thing. We hadn't even been gone a week and already the house felt stale and airless, as if our lives there were part of a past long distant.

I shivered and pushed on into the house, leaving that train of thought behind me. Forward was the only way to move now, and standing frozen in grief or fear wouldn't get me anywhere.

I moved like a shadow through the darkened living room to the master bedroom, into the walk-in closet. I used no lights; if I had been lucky enough to make it here without Katarovski's men discovering me, I wasn't going to take a chance on blowing it now.

Stretching my arms up over my head, I felt around on the high shelf that ran around the top of the closet. Somewhere up here...

My hand bumped into a familiar pebbled plastic case, and I pulled it down.

Inside this unassuming black case was my sole

concession to the horror I had survived over a year ago; an item I had bought shortly after Alexis and I got married. It was a Sig Sauer P250, a .357 caliber semi-automatic pistol, with three extra fully loaded clips. In all the months I had owned it, the only use the pistol had seen was target practice at the shooting range once a week.

Tonight all that would change. There was just no way I was going to walk into whatever was going on at Alexei's place without the Sig Sauer by my side.

I carried my purse and my gun case out to the garage, past Alexis's white Jaguar to my little blue Toyota. The Jag was a joy to drive, but the car was a local icon, as well known in Newton as the man who drove it.

The drive over to Alexei's villa wasn't very long. I had hoped to strike upon a fantastic plan for freeing him before I arrived, but as I sat in my car parked a few houses down the block, watching the sun dip behind the Spanish tile roof of my father-in-law's home turned prison, I had to admit I had nothing. No fantastic plan, no possible plan, not a faint glimmer of a plan of any sort.

I unlatched the gun case and jammed the extra clips into the pockets of my jeans. It made my jeans lumpy and uncomfortable. Surely I wouldn't need more than the fourteen rounds currently in the pistol--but I wasn't going to take the chance.

The Sig Sauer's weight was familiar and comforting in my hand, but I checked the safety and put it in my purse. I didn't like the idea of anyone glancing out of their window and seeing me packing it down the street.

The street seemed especially long that evening. I walked

briskly, trying not to focus on the enormity of what I had set out to do. The only advantage I had was that they certainly would not expect me to charge in alone like this--it was insane.

Alexei's villa was surrounded by a tall wrought iron fence that was designed more for beauty than security, judging by how easy it was for me to climb over it at the back of the property. I figured his captors were most likely to be in the front of the house, near the living room and the kitchen--not so much in the back of the house, which was all bedrooms and laundry.

The key was the central courtyard. The villa was a white-washed adobe rectangle, laid out around the central open-air courtyard--almost all of the rooms opened out onto it. If I could get into that courtyard undetected, I would be able to go anywhere I needed to from there.

Alexei had given Alexis and me both keys to the villa soon after we got married. The back door opened nearly silently into the laundry room. Inside, it was cool, and dark, and completely empty. That was the good news.

The bad news was that the laundry room did not have an exit to the courtyard. There were doors on either side of the room, and I had no idea what rooms they went to.

So I picked the door on the right, gritted my teeth, and threw it open.

No shouts or gunfire greeted me, so I went through. This room was brighter than the last, thanks to the glass sliding door to my left. A large four-poster bed dominated this room, with a low, wide dresser topped by a mirror on the far wall. The air felt solemn and time itself seemed to pass more slowly here, with a heavier gait.

The entire room screamed *master bedroom* as plainly as if the words had been painted on the wall. I felt acutely uncomfortable there, and turned for the sliding door so quickly I nearly ran into the tall chest of drawers next to me. Right in front of my face on top of the chest was an 8x10 photo in an ornate wooden frame.

I knew time was not on my side. I knew I needed to hurry, to keep moving. I could hear the urgency like a drumbeat, like a hammer pounding in my head.

But I couldn't walk on past this. I couldn't have said why, but I knew I needed to see this picture. I picked the frame up and tilted it toward the faint light creeping through the glass door. The photo was clearly not studio work; this was a snapshot someone had enlarged. There were four people in the picture--in the middle was a much younger Alexei, in a concert tuxedo, with an arm around a slim blonde woman in a headscarf, holding a blonde baby. She beamed at the camera--Elena Bruskalov, I was sure, holding baby Natalya.

Alexei's other arm was across the shoulders of another man in a concert tuxedo, holding a violin. Even without the graying hair and many extra wrinkles, I recognized the craggy face of Dmitri Kast.

It kind of took my breath away, looking into the smiling face of the man who had sacrificed himself to get us all back here. It brought a tear to my eye. It was a viciously effective reminder of one reason why I had to keep going.

I replaced the photo on the chest of drawers and let myself out into the courtyard. I could tell from the light spilling through the far windows that I had been right;

everyone seemed to be in the dining room. I moved across the grassy courtyard as quickly and quietly as I could, hoping to get a feel for how things were inside before any of them saw me.

The far side of the courtyard had a pretty landscaped feature, with a little pond surrounded by flowerbeds, and a dogwood tree leaning over the whole thing. Nearby was a concrete birdbath I had seen on my first visit there, sculpted into the shape of a little girl with a watering can. I knelt down behind the birdbath; between it and the shadows from the tree, I was concealed pretty well--nobody would see me there at a casual glance.

One of the Katarovski suits had already made himself comfortable at Alexei's big dining table, with the chair pushed back on two legs and his feet up on the table's shiny surface. I could see Alexei down at the foot of the table, tied securely to one of his own chairs.

As I watched, the second suit came in from the kitchen, carrying two big plates piled with sandwiches and potato chips. Apparently being an unscrupulous bully worked up quite an appetite.

He walked over to Alexei, and I sat up a little taller than I probably should have, in tense anticipation. Maybe they were going to untie him, to let him eat. Having Alexei free to move could only make my job easier.

Unfortunately it wasn't to be. The man in the suit just waved his plate under Alexei's nose, tormenting him with the smell of the food, then took the meals to the table, laughing. He handed one of the plates to his partner, and they both dug in.

Man, every time I saw one of these guys, he immediately gave me some horrible new reason to hate them all. Where had Petrov Katarovski rounded up so many completely heartless human beings, willing to do whatever soul-shredding thing he commanded of them for nothing more than a wage?

I reached into my purse and palmed the Sig, studying the situation behind the sliding glass door. I was determined to get through this with the least amount of bloodshed possible--a couple of stiffs turning up in the Bruskalov home would cause headaches for all of us.

A pity that the bad guys didn't seem to be constrained by such worries.

A television sat on the buffet against the far wall. The thugs must have brought it in from some other room-- Alexei had never kept a television in the dining room any time I had visited this house before. They had tuned it to a twenty-four hour news channel, and as I watched a line of text scrolled by in the headline bar that took my breath away.

"Extradition papers for Alexis Brooks received, approved. Extradition imminent, state department says."

Crap, crap, *crap*. I had known things were moving abnormally fast. I had known I didn't have much time. But I had never realized things were moving *so* abnormally fast, that I had *so* little time. It didn't even seem possible. Exactly how many strings could Petrov Katarovski pull?

Exactly a whole lot more than I had thought. I had to get moving, and pray that I wasn't already too late.

I raised the pistol and sighted carefully on the man who had teased Alexei with food, exhaled, and squeezed the trigger. If I missed this shot, it was as good as over.

I was up and moving before the sound of the shot had cleared. It shattered the glass in the door, caught the suit in the shoulder, and knocked him out of his chair.

The second agent leaped to his feet and reached for his shoulder holster, but I already had the Sig trained on him, and he froze.

I stepped carefully in through the jagged, gaping remains of the sliding door. "Take your jacket off. Unbuckle that holster, place it on the floor, and slide it to me. If you touch your gun--if I even think you are going to touch your gun--I will shoot you where you stand."

Maybe he had heard about the untimely end of his comrade in Zwickau. Maybe the Sig Sauer was just that intimidating. In any case, he removed the holster with exaggerated care, and slid it across the floor to me. I took out the pistol--some sort of large-caliber revolver I didn't inspect too closely--and jammed it into my waistband.

"Untie him," I commanded, jerking my chin in Alexei's direction.

While he complied, I disarmed the wounded man writhing on the floor.

When Alexei was free, we turned a couple of chairs back-to-back and tied the men into them, securing their arms to the arms of the chairs as well. I had no doubt some of their other suit friends would come save them.

I only hoped Alexei and I would be long gone when it happened.

♫

Before we left, I snagged one of the plates off the table,

tossed aside the one sandwich wedge that had been partially eaten, and passed the plate to Alexei. "You'd better take this. I don't know when you might have another chance to eat."

He nodded, took the plate, and stared at the food as if he had no earthly idea what to do with it.

Shell-shocked. And with good reason.

I set the safety on my Sig and both revolvers, and dumped them all into my purse, along with the extra clips I had in my pockets.

You know, three handguns and three clips full of .357 caliber ammunition makes for a pretty heavy purse.

I took Alexei's arm and pulled him towards the foyer. We hurried out of the house and down the dark street in silence.

I was guiding the Toyota out of my parking spot by the curb before Alexei spoke. "Chrispen, what is happening?"

I shook my head. "I don't even know where to start, Alexei, except to say that almost everything you've heard about it was a lie."

He nodded, considering. "So Alexis never abducted this Katarovski woman. That was a story to conceal whatever actually happened. That was the purpose of these men as well? To keep Alexis from revealing the truth?"

"Yes."

"I see. And what is this truth that the Katarovski's are so desperate to conceal?"

I sighed. "I am really not the one who should be telling you this. But after what you have been through, you deserve to know why. I don't know how to say it but bluntly--Irena Katarovski is actually your daughter, Natalya."

Alexei's complexion turned suddenly pasty. "What?"

"I'm sorry she couldn't be here to tell you herself. She risked everything to contact Alexis and I, to tell us. And Petrov Katarovski is risking everything to stop her."

Alexei sat back in his seat. "I see." There was a moment of quiet in the little car while he thought that through. "Not to be insensitive, *dorogaya,* but have you considered the possibility that this woman may be playing you false? Perhaps she is angry with her father and does this thing for revenge. Or perhaps this is but a clever ploy for publicity for Petrov Katarovski."

"I can't blame you for being cautious," I said, "or even suspicious, given who we are dealing with. But there is no doubt. It's funny, you know, that you call me dorogaya. That is what Dmitri Kast calls her. He stayed behind, fighting Katarovski family bodyguards, so that we could make it here." I paused, remembering. "She has your eyes."

"My eyes." Alexei fell silent.

I reached into my purse, and fumbled my way past the assortment of handguns to my cell phone. I wasn't sure what to do now--for Alexei's rescue to matter, Alexis and Natalya had to know about it so they could start spilling beans. But Alexis was in state custody--I was hardly going to be able to ring him up on his cell phone. I couldn't say for sure where Natalya was, but it looked like she was my only hope. If she had gone to Washington with Alexis for questioning, maybe she could get word to him that it was time to blow the lid off. Short of being telepathic, it was my best shot.

"Hello?" Natalya had been slower to answer than usual-- probably not a good sign.

"Natalya, great news. I have Alexei, and he is safe."

"That is great news." She didn't sound particularly enthused, and her voice was very quiet, as though she feared being overheard. "Unfortunately it comes a slight bit too late."

"What? What do you mean?"

"Alexis is already on a plane back to Germany. Petrov and I are aboard too, along with the Federal Minister of Justice. I had to run to the bathroom to take your call."

"The Federal Minister of Justice?" I echoed with growing dread. "From Germany?"

"In person," she said emphatically, as if that made the situation all the more dire. I realized belatedly that it probably did. It was a bad sign if a highly placed government official could be coerced into inconveniencing themselves by personally handling something like this.

"That's not good."

"You have a positive gift for understatement," Natalya said dryly. "I'm finding it difficult to imagine how things could be much more 'not good.'"

"Hey, at least I got Alexei away from them," I said defensively. I glanced over and found the man himself nibbling on one of the sandwiches. Good--it was beginning to sound as though we were in for a long night.

"That is true." She sounded thoughtful all of the sudden. "It may yet prove useful. Once we arrive in Germany, it will take time for them to get things started. We may find an opportunity for Alexis or me to speak out."

"Where are you going?"

"Where else? They are taking Alexis to Berlin, so of

course that is where Petrov and I will go as well. He's full of fury, feeding the press with stories of his ever-burning rage for those who would harm his precious daughter. It's all calculated, but it appears to be gaining him support."

I made a sound of disgust. "A true politician. Exactly where will they be taking Alexis in Berlin?"

"Custody," she said shortly. "Why--you can't be thinking of seeing him?"

Actually it was pretty close to the only thought in my mind. "Yes."

"Chrispen, you can't do that! You may not have been named for extradition, but don't think you won't be arrested if you show up there."

"Natalya, he's my husband."

She sighed. "I know that. But how much help will you be for him, locked in a cell of your own?"

"He needs to know his father is safe." My tone was low; I could hear the heaviness of defeat in my own voice.

"I will get word to him as soon as I can. It is risky, but not as much as for you."

It was my turn to sigh. Poor Natalya--she risked so much to try to keep us safe. "Hang in there, Natalya. We will be on a plane right behind you."

I dropped the phone back in my purse, and headed for the airport, as fast as I could get away with. I had to catch them before anything game-changing happened, and I had to disable this latest trap.

But more than that, I needed to end this definitively, once and for all.

I just wished I could figure out a way to do it.

♫

Alexei was dozing in the passenger seat when my cell phone rang. Caller information had been blocked; in deference to the current mad situation and to keep the ringer from disturbing Alexei, I broke my own rule and answered it. "Hello?"

"Mrs. Brooks, I have attempted twice to dissuade you from your course. The current situation saddens me, because it could have been avoided entirely if you had but listened to me."

I frowned. Two attempts? I didn't know who--

In my mind I suddenly connected the phone call back home with the letter at the hotel. Hadn't the name on that letter also turned up in Natalya's story? "Is this Anya Katarovski?"

She hesitated. I didn't blame her; if I had been in her position, I would have wanted to be anonymous, too. "Yes. You have not followed my advice."

"That's because your advice has been unfailingly awful!" I darted a glance at Alexei, and fought to keep my voice down. "Give up, go home, walk away from the job Alexis signed on to do."

"No job is worth breaking a family." Each word had a bitter little edge.

That comment did it--the gloves were off now. "Is that so? Mighty interesting to hear you say that, considering how little problem you had busting up families thirty years ago."

"What Petrov did, he did for love. In my grief I could not see it then."

"Oh, and it makes sense now? Look, Anya, I hate to

break it to you, but what I do I also do out of love. That's my husband you people are setting up for sacrificial slaughter."

"Husbands can be replaced," she said calmly. "You are young, you will find another. You are only related to the traitor Bruskalov through your man--your losses will be minimal. Irena is my only daughter."

"She's not your daughter," I said. "You must know that."

"Do you think you can raise a child from a toddler and not love her as your own?" She sounded angry. "Do you think for a moment she does not regard us as her parents? This is just a rebellious phase. I am begging you, for the sake of my family, to drop this thing. I can compensate you however you wish. I will pay anything to protect them."

This woman sickened me. She talked like I was the threat here--and she offered me *money?* To sell out Alexis?

She thought he could be *replaced?*

I felt like my head exploded. "Listen carefully, Anya, there are a few things you need to understand. Natalya is not your daughter--"

"Her name is Irena and *she is my daughter!*"

"--and whatever you may think about your husband, I will never, ever abandon mine. Not to you, not to your wretched husband, not to the very hounds of hell themselves. There is only one good way out of this for you-- stop this insanity, release Alexis, and let the truth be told."

"NEVER!" She shrieked at me like a banshee.

"So be it," I said. "On your own head be it, then--I will fight however I must to help my husband."

I clicked my cell phone shut with a trembling hand.

"Was that Anya Katarovski?" Alexei asked quietly.

I sighed. "I'm sorry, Alexei. I didn't mean to wake you. Yes, that was her. She's batshit crazy, Alexei--just like her husband."

Alexei frowned. "That does not bode well for us, to have to face such people, does it?"

"No." I clenched the steering wheel in my hands until my knuckles turned white.

It didn't bode well at all.

Alexei had to be dead on his feet. With those suits holding him prisoner in his own home, saturated with disdain for one they considered a traitor, who knew how long it had been since he had eaten well or slept properly? I figured he would be asleep as soon as the plane was in the air. I figured we would both be asleep.

I was wrong. When the mad steep rush of takeoff leveled, I glanced over at him, and found him running his fingers over a news magazine he'd bought at the airport. The magazine had a long article about Irena Katarovski and her alleged abduction, with several photographs. I knew that story had to be why Alexei had wanted the magazine, but now he seemed almost afraid to open it.

"I understand," he said softly, "that Irena Katarovski is a member of the Maestri Soviet."

"Yes." I wondered if that pleased him, that in spite of everything that had been done her, his daughter had found her way into the orchestra Alexei's father had founded. It was like fate, operating on a level far beyond anything Petrov Katarovski could influence, or even touch, and it gave me hope for all of us. "She plays the viola."

"Viola," he said, and laughed. I wondered if he was remembering, as I was, Alexis's fondness for viola jokes.

"Yes. She wasn't permitted to play the violin. She very nearly wasn't allowed to study viola. The Katarovski's were very worried about being found out, I think."

"I should imagine so." He flipped a page in the magazine. "Is she any good?"

"I've never heard her play, but my impression is that she is. They keep her in the middle of the section deliberately to keep her from drawing attention."

Alexei studied a picture in the magazine, of the woman the world called Irena Katarovski holding her viola in front of her and looking pensive, her gaze lowered.

"She looks like her mother," he whispered, touching the blonde hair, the pale face. "So much like her mother."

"Except for her eyes," I said. "She has your eyes."

"So I hear." He closed the magazine and smiled at me, but it was a shaky smile. "Can we really do this, *dorogaya?* Or am I about to lose both of my children, for good?"

I patted his hand, trying my best to be confident and reassuring. "We can do this, Alexei, and we will. We'll get them both back."

I turned to the little window beside me, hoping to see moonlight on the clouds to bolster my flagging spirits. But the sky was dark and all I could see in the window was my own ghostly reflection, wide-eyed and so very alone.

MOVEMENT THREE:
Endgame

We had a three-hour layover in Paris. Under other circumstances, Paris was a city I would have loved to visit. But right now, time was working against me, and an airport was an airport was an airport. I'd seen far too many of them lately.

I couldn't stomach the thought of food, and Alexei wasn't hungry, so we picked up a couple cups of coffee and sat down in the departure lounge, prepared to defeat this layover through the brute force method of waiting, camped out in one spot.

I had no more than gotten settled in my seat when my cell phone chimed, notifying me of an incoming text message.

> I see that you need some incentive to see things my way. Consider the attached, just sent to me by one of my bodyguards. Save one or save the other--you cannot have both. I know you will do the right thing.
>
> --Anya

The attachment gave me a chill. It was a picture of my mother's house in North Carolina. There was a timestamp--I quickly did the timezone conversions and found that this picture was only an hour old.

Agents? At my mother's house?

I stared unseeingly at the phone in my hand. This was the threat Anya counted on to bring me to my knees--she didn't know or care that Alexei was free. This threat was for me and me alone. *Save your mother or save your husband--you cannot have both.*

"We'll see about that," I muttered, dialing a number on my speed dial.

"Hello?"

"Mom? Mom, is that you? It's Chrispen."

Her laugh eased my worries; whatever was going on outside, it had not affected my mother--yet. "Of course it's me, dear, who else would it be? But Chrispen, what is going on with you? I've seen the most disturbing things on the news lately...and you haven't called at all..."

I bit my lip. "I'm sorry--things have been a bit hectic. It's a very long story."

"I've got time," she said.

"No, you don't. Look, Mom, everything you have seen on television is a lie. The people who are accusing us are trying to divert attention from themselves--they've done us a great deal of harm. And they aren't done yet. But now, it looks like they are after you as well."

"What?"

"They've just sent me some evidence that suggests they are keeping watch on your house."

"Oh, my. Chrispen, what should I do?"

"First, try not to freak out too much. As weird as it sounds this isn't really about you--they are trying to use you as leverage to control what I do.'"

"Well, screw that!" she said bluntly.

I laughed. "I agree. So here's what we need to do--we have got to get you out of there while they are waiting to see what I do. But they can't see you go. Leave the lights and the television on, leave everything like it is right now. Go out back--maybe take the watering can, like you're going to take care of your flowers. You are going to have to go over the back fence, into the neighbor's yard. Get to their back door. Tell them your car won't run and there's a family emergency--get them to drive you to Uncle Jim's place--or call you a taxi if they just won't drive you."

"You want me to go to Jim's?"

"Yes. Tell him you're in danger--tell him there might be

trouble. He needs to keep his shotgun handy, and he needs to not be afraid to use it if any men in dark suits start sniffing around."

"Men in dark suits. Got it." She hesitated. "Chrispen, are you sure about this?"

"Positive. Go now, and once you start moving, move fast. Don't slow down, don't hesitate. And don't leave Uncle Jim's until I come for you, no matter what you hear or see. When Alexis and I show up, you'll know it's safe. I love you, Mom."

"I love you too, dear. Good luck."

"To you, too."

I sat in the quiet departure lounge after the call, my mind racing but not getting anywhere. I could only hope this crazy scheme worked.

Alexei laid a gentle hand on my shoulder. "Your mother will be fine."

"Thanks," I said. "I know."

But even as I said the words, I couldn't quite believe them.

♫

The airport in Berlin was bright and clean and impossibly alive. The very atmosphere of the place was hopelessly at odds with our moods--Alexei and I were practically zombies by that point. We staggered mindlessly along with the flow of people leaving the plane, until we looked around and found ourselves alone in a pretty well deserted boarding gate. It was just the empty rows of plastic seats and us: the living, walking dead. We must have been a joy to behold.

"We need to find out what they've done with Alexis," I said, trying to force my brain to work properly. "That's got to come first--find out where Alexis is."

"There," Alexei said, pointing behind me and over my head.

I whirled around. There on the wall was a flat-screen television set showing my husband in a colorless jumper, his wrists cuffed together, locked in a holding cell. I couldn't understand the German voice-over, but I assumed they were talking about the extradition. The words didn't matter anyway. It was the eyes--Alexis's empty, hollow eyes--that haunted me, devoid of any of the humor or fire that I loved so well.

As I watched, Alexis slowly turned his back to the camera without a word. If I had only had some way to contact him, he could have been using the opportunity to make his own defense.

The footage cut suddenly to Petrov Katarovski, clutching Natalya's hand like a lifeline, surrounded by cameras and microphones and agents in dark suits.

"Yes," he said, smiling like a man who had just won the lottery, "I had to come as soon as I heard they apprehended the monster who had my girl. I can't tell you how happy I am that she is safe."

He was speaking English. Why would a Russian man on German television speak English?

"Moreover," he continued, "I am so very distressed to learn that Brooks's second wife is missing. Right on the heels of my daughter's abduction, too. I do so fervently hope no foul play has befallen her."

He directed his gleaming smile right into the camera, and I figured it was clear enough why he chose to speak in English. No matter. His threats would not deter me, no matter what language delivered them.

"I'd like to take this opportunity," Natalya said--

--and the merest hint of a frown flickered across Katarovski's face--

--and Natalya collapsed into the arms of the agent behind her.

"My daughter is not yet recovered from her ordeal," Katarovski said quickly. "This excitement, it is too much for her. No more questions. Later, perhaps."

He barreled through the crowd without a backward glance, followed by a pair of suits, one of whom was carrying Natalya.

The television cut back to the news desk, where the anchors discussed this development rapidly and in German.

I swung back around to face Alexei. "What just happened?"

Alexei shook his head, frowning. "I don't know. But that fainting, that was suspicious."

"Just a bit." I glanced over my shoulder at the television, but it seemed to be out of useful information. I took a deep breath and rubbed my temples, trying hard to think clearly. "Okay. We can't do anything more here. I guess the first thing we need to do is go find a place to stay."

We left the gate, hurrying toward the surface train boarding.

But in my mind all I could see was Alexis, in prisoner

fatigues and two days's worth of stubble, turning his back to reporter's cameras.

♪

It was probably a reflection on my sheltered life, but I was surprised to find Best Western hotels in Germany. There were at least three of them in Berlin itself. Perhaps out of a fervent desire for home and normality, I picked one of those to stay in instead of something native to the country.

We were both half-starved and dead on our feet. I ordered in a couple of sandwich plates, and closed the heavy curtains against the bright afternoon sun.

By the time I turned back from the window, Alexei was crashed out, sprawled across one of the beds and snoring.

That was probably smart. If I'd had any sense I would have gone to sleep as well. But I was too anxious to even think about sleep, eaten up with worry and still mulling over the newsreel from the airport in the back of my mind.

So I grabbed one of the sandwich trays and made myself comfortable on the other bed. I turned on the television with the volume down low--I couldn't understand it anyway, I was just hoping to find a news channel for some distraction while I ate. Maybe I would even manage to decipher some clue about how things were going for Alexis, or learn some new bit of information about Natalya's sudden mysterious fainting fits.

Odd, that. Petrov implied that it was stress or excitement that caused her collapse. Alexis and I had been with her through some pretty dicey jams--certainly more stressful than any press conference--and she had never shown any sign of that sort of weakness.

But then we already knew that Katarovski would not hesitate to lie to further his own ends. This nervous fainting story had to be a cover for something else.

But what that something else could be--I had no ideas on that at all, nothing that even seemed like a good starting point for an idea.

Alexei's magazine lay on the nightstand. I picked it up and held it in front of me in the dim flickering light from the television. The entire front cover was a close-up photograph of a smiling Petrov Katarovski.

Natalya was right--Alexei was more handsome than this man. Katarovski's face was too long and narrow, with a chin too pointed and a goatee that lent a sinister look.

You wouldn't look at the man's carefully groomed face and spotless smile and think he was a psychotic murderer.

I grabbed the ballpoint pen sporting the Best Western logo from the nightstand and inked in a pair of horns, holding the finished piece at arm's length to gauge the full effect.

Now he looked like a murdering psycho. Now anyone could tell at a glance that this was the type of man who would have no problem destroying entire lives to cover his own arse. The type of man who could easily engineer my current situation.

The whole situation just stank--I didn't see how things could get much worse. Alexis was in government custody, awaiting trial for a crime he had not committed, forbidden to assert his own innocence. Natalya was still firmly in the clutches of the man who had systematically destroyed her family to get to her. And Alexei and I were nearby but utterly useless, with no apparent way to stop this snowball as it rollicked on down the hill to hell. Katarovski seemed unstoppable, and he had me backed into a pretty tight corner.

And I hated to see a bad guy win.

Alexei shifted fitfully in his sleep on the other bed. "Elena," he said clearly, and one of his arms reached up as if of its own volition, his fingers straining as if to touch something they could not quite reach.

A moment later the hand fell back to his side and he slept peacefully once more, his face turned toward the curtained window.

It probably shouldn't have surprised me--it made sense that he would be upset right now, obsessing more than usual over the wife and daughter that had been stolen from him.

Elena, sadly, was beyond our reach, irrevocably gone from this world. But Natalya--after all these years he had a chance at having his daughter back again. A chance that right now seemed to depend on me finagling us all some way out of this impossible mess, some final solution as obvious and irrefutable as the distinctive set of eyes both of them shared.

And then it hit me, like walking dead into a 2x4 across a doorway because you were looking the other way. The problem was simple, and the solution was obvious. I wanted to prove Natalya's true parentage.

What I needed was a paternity test.

I grabbed the phone book out of the nightstand and started ringing up laboratories.

Now back home this situation would have been no problem. But I quickly found that Germany was a very different barrel of fish. The first two places I called didn't even want to talk to me, directing me briefly to consult with my physician before disconnecting the call.

The third lab I called was a bit more cooperative. The representative there told me that if I could come in, he would set me up with everything I needed to prepare for the test.

Next I called Natalya's cell phone. I didn't figure there was any way at all she would answer, but to my surprise she picked up on the second ring.

"Natalya! I didn't really expect to be able to talk to you."

"Petrov is in a meeting with a government official. I would tell you which one, but he went to some trouble to keep that information from me."

"Hmm. That is probably not a good sign."

"No, undoubtedly not." She sounded kind of aggravated. I supposed being kept cooped-up and helpless would have done the same thing to me. "What do you need?"

"Do you have a way to get over here? I have an idea that may help us, but I don't dare discuss it on the phone. Some things work better if no one sees them coming."

Natalya laughed. "Indeed. Transportation will not be a problem--when my so-called father meets with government puppets, *they* come drive *him*. So his car is here. And the bodyguards have been quite lax since we arrived--they think I am still toothless."

"You mean they don't know yet that Alexei is free?"

"Indeed. My father's conclusion is that you got too

scared--you'd had enough, saw your opportunity, and ran for it."

"Seriously? Katarovski thinks I would just cut my losses and run, that I would just abandon Alexis to this?"

"He believes Alexis, too, when he says he has no idea where you are or what you are doing." Natalya paused. "Of course, at this point, he probably doesn't."

For some reason it bothered me, that Petrov Katarovski thought I would just leave. Alexis needed me more right now than he ever had before in his life--there was no conceivable way I would turn my back. But why should I care what Katarovski thought? The man was no friend of mine. And he was completely morally bankrupt.

"I'll leave you to ponder that then," Natalya said, disconcerted by my silence. "Where are you staying?"

"It's a Best Western," I said. I picked up the little postcard from the nightstand and read her the address.

"Oh, that's not too far. Give me ten minutes."

We disconnected, and I turned to regard my father-in-law, still sacked out. The phone call hadn't disturbed him at all. I considered waking him, but it seemed cruel, now that he was finally getting some rest. I also didn't want to raise his hopes--there was every chance that Natalya was going to show me some perfectly obvious reason why this wouldn't work, and shoot the whole thing down.

So instead I grabbed my key card and my purse and went out to sit in front of the hotel and wait for Natalya. We would bring Alexei up to speed when it looked like everything would work out.

Of course, sitting there right then, it seemed like the

height of optimistic folly to imagine there would ever again be a moment when it looked like things were going to work out.

♬

Petrov Katarovski's car wasn't hard to recognize--it would have been harder to miss, the way it jumped out at you and wrestled your eyeballs to the ground with sheer arrogance. It was a classic Rolls Royce, long and shiny, and probably very elegant until the exterior had been attacked with panels of wood veneer, and copious amounts of gold colored trim applied to every conceivable location. Even the headlight casings were gold. The front grill was entirely gold colored metal, and when the sun hit it, it could have struck a person blind. The side view mirror, the bumper, the trim around the windows and inside the wheels all gleamed gold. Even the Rolls Royce Spirit of Ecstasy on the hood was a brassy gold color. The parts that weren't wood-grain or gold metal were white. If the entire car had been that white, with regular chrome accents, the car would have been breathtakingly beautiful. As it was--it was breathtaking, all right. On the hood of the car, in gold paint, was a scripty, stylized K surrounded by a circular wreath motif. There just weren't words for it. It was the glittery gold icing on the butt-ugly cake.

All of the windows in the car were tinted dark black. I could only assume it was to prevent embarrassment or criminal charges to the people inside.

I gaped at it in a kind of shock, until I regained my wits and let myself in to the passenger seat of the car.

"I know," Natalya said miserably. "It really is hideous,

isn't it? This was a perfectly beautiful 1947 Silver Wraith, right up until Petrov Katarovski got a hold of it. What can I say? It is the only vehicle I had access to."

I handed Natalya a slip of hotel stationery. The interior of the car was still lovely, with a beautiful walnut burl woodgrain dash. In my mind I ticked off the list of crimes I knew Petrov Katarovski to be responsible for. There was no question; this car had to be added to that list.

"What's this?" Natalya demanded, squinting at my handwriting scrawled on the little page. "An address? Is this where we need to go?"

I nodded. "It's a lab. I'm interested in a paternity test for you, to prove beyond question who your father actually is."

Natalya pulled the rolling monstrosity out onto the road, frowning. "Do you think it will really be that easy?"

"I don't see why it should. Nothing else has been. But we have to try. It's the first time you and Alexei have been in the same country in decades."

Natalya bit her lip and nodded. "We should be there soon."

"Good." I couldn't help feeling we were on borrowed time with this little excursion--the only question was whose absence would be discovered first, Natalya's or mine. "I hope you won't think I'm prying...but Alexei and I saw you on television today. What's with this fainting business? When did that start?"

"Fainting." She said the word like it was dirty. "Not hardly. The bodyguard standing next to me jammed a needle into my hip. I don't know what was in it, but it was very effective. I was unconscious before I could even cry out."

I stared at her in open horror. "They are giving you drugs to keep you from talking?"

Natalya nodded grimly. "Remember, they were planning to kill you and Alexis to keep you quiet. I don't think they are prepared to go that far with me--I'm too important to them--but we are all in danger. That will never change, unless this plan of yours succeeds."

I didn't answer. What was there to say? Everything she had said was true, which was why this had to work. I was determined to make this work, to get us all out of this. Unfortunately, Petrov Katarovski was equally determined I should fail, and he had money, people, resources, and support.

The lab was an unassuming place, concrete and blocky with few windows. The room we stepped into could hardly be called a lobby; it was very small and very bright, with white walls and a stainless steel counter along the back of the room. The counter was topped by white, opaque glass that extended to the ceiling. A single clear window was open in the middle, and behind that was a young man in glasses and a white lab coat. The whole room seemed sterile and very off-putting.

"Hello," I said hesitantly, "I need to talk to someone about a--"

"Paternity test?" finished the young man, looking at me over the tops of his glasses. "I'm Scott Nichols." He stuck his hand out to me through the little window. "I spoke to you on the phone."

"Scott, hello." I shook his hand. "I am Chrispen Brooks. This is Natalya. She is the one whose parentage we would like to prove."

"I see." Scott reached up to a shelf that was just out of our view and pulled down a little white box. "You will find everything you need in here. I should point out that in Germany a paternity test requires the written consent of both parents. The form in the box is set up to handle this--just have them both sign it, and you'll be set."

"My mother is dead," Natalya said darkly.

"Oh--I--I'm so sorry. You can just write 'deceased' on the line for her signature, then."

"When can we pick up the results?" I asked.

"Oh, it's a very fast test. We ship them all over the world for next-day results. You'll be able to pick up yours in the morning. We open at six."

"Terrific!" I told him. The sooner we had hard results in our hands, the better. I regarded this as our insurance policy of sorts against whatever move Katarovski might make next.

And as we paid the fee, collected the white box, and hurried back to the ugly-mobile, the thought of an insurance policy made me feel a little better. But only a little.

Because the thing about insurance is, you never know when you'll be required to draw on it.

♪

It only took me a moment to retrieve the hotel key card from my purse. But you'd have thought it took an hour, the way Natalya fidgeted, fussing with her hair and dancing from foot to foot in apparent agitation.

"What has got you so worked up?" I demanded.

She shot me a look of purest impatience and belatedly, I

understood.

"Hey, look," I said. "This is nothing to tie yourself in knots over. He's been waiting just as long for you. He would probably be just as nervous, if he knew you were out here."

Natalya glared at me.

"Yeah, that didn't help at all. What I mean to say is this. Think about everything you have been through lately--the running, the dodging, the rescuing and escaping...if you can take all of that then meeting your real father should be a piece of cake, right?"

"Just open the door," she said through gritted teeth, in a tone that tried very hard to strangle me for her.

So rather than stick my foot any farther in my mouth, I shut up and opened the door. "Alexei?" I called, stepping into the room. "I'm back. And I've brought company."

He was standing on the far side of the room, looking out of the window. "Ah, *dorogaya,* there you are. I was just wondering when I should call the--"

He turned around and caught sight of us and froze, the color draining from his face.

"I'm sorry," I said, crossing the room with Natalya close behind me. "I know this is sudden--I should have called, I just thought you might still be asleep, and--"

"Chrispen?" Natalya said quietly.

I turned to her in surprise; she wasn't even looking at me. "Yes?"

"Hush."

She was right, my awkward monologue wasn't making anything any better. I stepped back and shut up.

Alexei stared like he couldn't believe his eyes, frozen in

place by shock. Natalya studied him a moment, tears welling up in her eyes, and then she was a blur of motion, flinging herself into his arms and dealing him a crushing hug around the neck.

"N--Natalya?" Alexei said, and his voice broke.

"I have dreamed of this moment for so many years," she said, clinging to him as though he might evaporate.

"As have I," Alexei said.

I let myself out of the room and helped myself to a plastic chair that probably should have been over by the pool. This reunion would go better without my clumsy efforts to mediate, and for some reason it was making me melancholy. It didn't make sense--hadn't we all of us fought long and hard so this moment could happen? But there it was. Alexis's absence from that moment felt physical and real, a great gaping hole with jagged edges and no bottom, and it was in my chest, in my very soul. A hole like that is easier to bear in solitude. I wrapped my arms tight around myself, watching children splash in the hotel pool, and tried to tell myself it wouldn't be like this for long. I would have test results in hand in the morning--cold, hard, irrefutable proof--and somehow I would make this nightmare be over. Somehow I would get Alexis back again, and our lives would be what they were before we had ever heard of Zwickau or Irena or Petrov Katarovski.

Somehow.

I don't know how long I sat there, lost in a kind of thought that precluded all sense of time. Eventually I heard the slight sound of the door latch operating behind me, and turned to see Alexei standing in the doorway.

"Chrispen? Are you all right?"

I nodded, wiping under my eyes with my thumbs. It had never been part of my plan to go sit alone and cry, but then when did things ever go according to my plans? "I'm sorry. I just--I miss him, Alexei. I miss him more than I can say."

"Ach." He knelt down beside my chair and put his arm around my shoulders. "Don't cry, *dorogaya*. You've been very brave."

"Do you think so? I sure don't feel very brave."

"Look at everything you have done since this began," he said. "Against the odds, we are all still here. That, as they say, is no mean feat."

It was true, we had walked a pretty narrow line to make it this far. It didn't really make me feel better right then, though. I sniffled and wiped my eyes again.

"Natalya tells me you have a plan," he said.

"*Plan* is a pretty strong word." I stood up, and together we went back into the hotel room. Natalya sat in a chair by the window, holding the white box on her lap. She handed it to me, pretending not to notice my puffy red eyes the same way I pretended not to notice hers.

"What's that?" Alexei asked in a tone of exaggerated curiosity, probably to keep either of us from bursting into tears again.

I chuckled. "This is everything we need to order a paternity test for Natalya."

He looked at the box, and back at me. "Why didn't we think of that before?"

I shrugged. "When have we had time? Katarovski and his agents have made sure we are always on the run, without two spare minutes to stop and consider our options. This is the first break I've had."

"That is only because he did not count on your dogged persistence," Natalya said, and the way she said it, it sounded like a compliment. "Petrov is used to those who bend easily to his will, who run and hide when he threatens them. He thinks you are one more such person."

"Then he is in for a surprise," I said, spreading the contents of the box on the table. "I'm not very brave, and I'm not very smart, and I'm not very good at this. But I will never stop fighting him."

"Nor I," Natalya said.

"And I as well," Alexei said.

Collecting cheek swabs, storing and labeling them, and filling out the requisition form only took a few minutes. A few painless minutes to put an end to years of lies and broken families. It was overwhelming to contemplate.

Alexei wanted to go back to the lab with us. I think on some level he worried that once she left his sight, his daughter would disappear again. And who could blame him? I couldn't even say for certain it wasn't true.

But I still had to convince him to stay behind. Alexei Bruskalov was far better known than I was, and much more recognizable. The last thing we needed was for him to be spotted, especially while Katarovski still believed him to be out of the picture back in Ohio.

So in the end it was Natalya and I who took the white box back to the desecrated Rolls Royce, and from there back to the lab.

"It will be ready in the morning?" I pressed Scott as he

unpacked the box.

"Absolutely," he said, holding the plastic specimen containers up to the light. "Everything looks great."

"I still can't believe this is going to work," Natalya said. "After all these years...such a simple solution."

"It's going to work," I told her, turned for the door. "Petrov won't have a leg to stand on."

"Excuse me." I turned to find Scott watching us. He looked like he wasn't sure he should have spoken at all. "Forgive me, but--I gather her parentage is contested?"

I nodded. "There is a man who seems dead set on presenting himself to the world as her father. But he isn't."

"And this test you've submitted, this sample is from the true father?"

"That's right." I didn't see where he was going with this, but I was willing to hear him out. He had been nothing but helpful.

"Then, if I may make a suggestion, perhaps it would be wise to test the other man as well? To convince an unwilling party, a positive and a negative result together work far better than one alone."

My stomach sank.

Natalya immediately protested. "But the order form says this test is over ninety-nine percent accurate."

I closed my eyes and sighed. "No, Scott is right. I don't like it either. But you know Petrov will jump on any excuse to discredit the findings, and these tests have been wrong before, however rarely. It's the only way. We have to test him, too."

"We would need that gentleman's signature as well," Scott

said hesitantly, pushing another white box through the window. "If that is going to be a problem--"

"It is no problem," Natalya said. She scooped up the box, thanked Scott for his help, and we hurried back out to the car.

Natalya set the box between us on the seat. We both regarded it as though it might suddenly explode.

"Why did you tell him the signature was no problem?" I asked. "Petrov would more likely consent to death by firing squad than to this test."

"I've been faking his signature ever since I was in school," Natalya said, waving a hand dismissively. "He can't tell the difference himself. So signing the form really is not a problem. But the sample...I do not see how we can collect that. Do you have any ideas?"

"Lots," I said, "but none that are very likely to work. We sure aren't going to have any luck in public. We need to get the box into your hotel room--maybe you could manage it while he sleeps? Maybe--"

Natalya cut me off with a gasp that sounded genuinely painful. "Petrov! He's coming!" she hissed. Her face was ashen, her eyes frozen on the rearview mirror.

"Oh, no," I breathed, reaching instinctively for the door handle. "He can't find me here!"

"Stop!" Natalya held out a restraining hand, freezing me before I pushed the door open. "He is too close--there is no way you will get out of here without being seen."

For just a moment I stared at her, my brain crippled with horror, spinning its wheels but unable to gain any traction.

Then I turned and bailed over the back of the seat. A

heavy velour blanket was folded neatly on the back seat, monogrammed with the same ostentatious K and wreath that adorned the hood of the car. I shook the blanket out and threw it over myself, huddling on the floor in the little space between the front and back seat. Natalya poked the box under there with me.

"Whatever happens," came her low whisper, *"don't move."*

Funnily enough, I had worked out that much on my own. This was insanity--how could anyone possibly miss the untidy lump of blanket apparently wadded up on the floor of an otherwise spotless car? The only thing I had going for me was that Katarovski still believed me to be in America, prevented from any action by the threat he imagined still hung over Alexei's head. He had no reason to suspect any plot here--as far as he knew, we were all still right where he wanted us.

I heard the passenger door open, felt the car shake with the force of it. "Irena, my darling, what are you doing here?" Katarovski's voice made my ears itch. It wasn't the heavy accent--not so different from Natalya's, after all--it was more the way he spoke. Ever mindful of public opinion and the many passers-by, his tone was carefully, deliberately amiable. But underneath it was hard, unforgiving--underneath was a tone no father would use with a daughter he cared about. Slick and shiny, but deadly underneath, like a knife dipped in cooking oil, so was the man, and so was his voice. I tensed up just hearing him.

"Eating lunch, Father. There." I couldn't see Natalya, but could only assume she gestured to the cafe across the street. "I was just about to go back to the hotel."

"It's a bit late for lunch, don't you think?" I could hear the frown in Katarovski's voice. "And what have you done to my blanket? How can I be expected to use it when it has been treated in such a manner?"

"I am sorry." Natalya's tone was even. "I will fix it."

"See that you do." The car shifted, and I realized to my utter horror that Katarovski had seated himself. "Since you are on your way back anyway, you may take me with you."

If Natalya made any response to that, it was only an expression I was unable to see. Before I had reconciled myself to what was happening, the Rolls Royce glided smoothly out into the street, carrying me--a helpless stowaway, trapped with a man determined to destroy me and everyone I cared about.

So that was not one of the best situations I've ever been in. But at that point there was precious little I could do about it. I did the only thing I could do--I lay as still as a stone under the blanket, trying not to even breathe.

"How did you find me?" Natalya's voice in the driver's seat sounded merely curious, as though she was just making conversation.

"You can't think our guards would fail to notice your disappearance. Surely you do not imagine a car as magnificent as this one is difficult to locate, no matter the city?"

Natalya said nothing. I understood; I could feel the danger closing as well, but I couldn't tell from which side the attack would come.

"Viktor called me as soon as they located the car."

Katarovski's tone was deceptively mild. "He said the Brooks woman was here. Now tell me, my darling daughter, what might you have been doing with her?"

My heart stopped beating.

"Sitting. Eating." Natalya sounded completely unfazed. "Last time I checked, I was still permitted to do those things."

"Hmph. Go on."

Natalya sighed. "She only wanted to talk to me. She was desperate to find out where Alexis is, what is happening to him. I did not think it would hurt to tell her that much."

"You rarely think at all." Katarovski sighed. "Why were you still there, sitting alone in the car, if your desperate friend was gone? You seem nervous, Irena."

"Do I?" She certainly didn't sound nervous. She sounded almost bored, like nothing Petrov Katarovski could say or do or think or feel could ever interest her in the slightest. "I admit I am upset. It is distressing, speaking to her. She loves her husband very much."

"Hmph. Perhaps she and her much-loved husband should have listened when they were warned."

Natalya didn't seem to have an answer for that. Truth be told, I didn't either. The only response I could conceive of was jumping up and strangling him to death. Alas, that course of action was doomed to failure, and I knew it. Still, the idea was strangely tempting.

Fortunately, I was not left to struggle with temptation overly long. The car pulled to a smooth stop, and doors opened.

"Take care of her, boy," Katarovski's voice said, clearly

from outside the car, "she is one of a kind. Come, Irena."

"That she is, sir," replied an unfamiliar voice from the driver's side of the car, whistling in disbelief. "That she certainly is."

The doors closed, and the car pulled slowly away. I forced myself to hold still, fighting with my rising alarm. Who was this man driving the car now? Where was he going with it? What on earth was going to become of me?

Even under the blanket, I could see the change in the light, could feel the transition in the pavement, as the car moved from daylight to indoors. It finally hit me--valet parking! This was an attendant parking the Rolls Royce. All I had to do was relax and be patient--which was much easier to do now that I had some grasp on the situation--and he would soon be gone.

What I was going to do then, though, I didn't yet know.

I ended up lying motionless in the car quite a bit longer than I probably needed to. I was convinced that as soon as I sat up, the valet would bring in another car, and I would be caught, busted, with no good explanation for how I had gotten there or what I was doing. But that kind of fear is only paralyzing for as long as you let it be. Eventually I had to remind myself that no matter how long I waited, there would still be the possibility of getting caught.

I pushed myself up off the floor, feeling sharp, stabbing protest in every joint. I sat down on the leather backseat, easing my head from side to side, rolling my shoulders, trying my best to loosen up my stiff, sore muscles.

I was in a parking garage. I had never stayed in a hotel

with valet parking or a parking garage before--just another way I was out of my element here. Surely I could find a taxi out on the street, and make it back to my own hotel.

Only, as I folded the velour blanket, keeping Natalya's promise for her, the white box rolled out and landed at my feet.

The white box! Honestly, in the fear and turmoil of stowing away, I had almost completely forgotten about the test--about the sample. Obtaining that sample seemed just as impossible now as it had half an hour ago. Maybe more, because Natalya was gone.

I so wanted to forget about it, to find myself a taxi and drop the box in a trash can on the way out. But I knew I couldn't do that. I could see so many bad endings to this whole insane adventure--there were so many ways this could all work out to me never seeing Alexis again. The one thing I was certain about: if I was going to get Alexis out of this, I needed every bit of ammunition I could get.

And a paternity test on Katarovski himself was very powerful ammunition indeed.

I sighed, grabbing the box. It didn't look like I really had any choice. Not if I ever hoped to see my husband alive again.

I stepped out of the Rolls Royce and closed the door behind me in one quick motion. I did not want to be seen with the car, and yet I made myself linger a moment longer, peering in the front window, hoping against hope Natalya had contrived to leave some clue that would help guide me.

No such luck. The front seat was bare.

It was on me, then. I turned away and surveyed the dim

parking garage over the tops of shiny, expensive, valet-parked cars. Beyond the ropes demarcating the valet section, beyond the common parking area, I could see the entrance to the hotel. I squared my shoulders and headed that direction.

What on earth was I going to do when I got there? Somehow I had to convince a desk clerk to tell me where the Katarovski's were staying. And that wasn't going to be easy.

I pushed the dividing rope down with my free hand and stepped over it, cradling the box against me so I wouldn't drop it.

The box. I glanced down at it--it was white, glossy cardboard, unlabeled. Perhaps I could pass it off as a package I needed to deliver to Katarovski.

The rest of the parking garage passed in a blur as I considered variations on that story that I might use. As I reached for the brass handle on the heavy glass door, I heard my cell phone chime from inside my purse.

I dug it out and flipped it open. There was a text message from Natalya.

Katarovski Suite--top floor, right side of hallway

Bless her! She had just saved me a lot of trouble.

I dropped my phone back in my purse, hauled the big door open, and strode into the hotel lobby is if I belonged there. The key in these sorts of situations is always confidence--behaving as if you know exactly where you are going and have a perfect right to be there. So I kept my shoulders back and my head high, walking neither too slow nor too fast, and praying no one would challenge me.

I was halfway across the spacious lobby, listening to the echoes of my hard-soled shoes off the tiled floor through the vaulted ceilings, when a door at the far end of the check-in counter flow open, banging into the wall behind it with a sharp sound that commanded the attention of everyone in the room. A frazzled-looking little man barreled through the door, chattering anxiously in German.

My grasp of the German language was pretty poor, but the words that I did know, I recognized even when spoken quickly by fluent speakers. I caught "manager", "emergency", and "camera".

And he spoke the name of Katarovski.

What was going on? I glanced over at the man, hoping to decipher more of the situation.

He looked my direction, and I saw his eyes widen. He jabbered even faster, gesturing wildly, pointing towards me.

Now that couldn't be good. I looked straight ahead and hurried on through the lobby, and around the corner to the elevators. The doors to the elevator slid open as I got there, and a portly gentleman stepped off, not even glancing at me as he passed.

The elevator was empty and open in front of me, with wood paneling and soft music; my ticket to the top floor. Not a single obstacle blocked my path.

And yet I hesitated. That ruckus in the lobby--I didn't know what was going on, but there was no question about it--that little man had gotten a whole lot more agitated when he saw me. Did I really want to be trapped in a moving car I couldn't control, with no way to know who or what would be on the other side of those doors when they opened again?

I walked on past the elevator and found a metal door with a long, narrow window in it, leading to the stairwell. With a quick glance at the deserted hall behind me, I went inside.

The stairs were concrete with a metal handrail. The plushness of the lobby was not to be seen here--it was plain most people never even saw this place. Guests used the big wood-paneled elevator, and staff must have had their own elevator, hidden somewhere from public view. The stairwell had an air of long disuse, as though they only kept it around to satisfy fire safety regulations.

So much the better. The hotel had six floors; the more of them I could pass unseen, the happier I would be. The fact that this hotel maintained a set of rooms they called the Katarovski Suite made me think I just might not be among friends.

I hurried up the stairs on the balls of my feet, trying to make as little noise as possible. Six flights of stairs doesn't sound like much, but I was pretty well winded when I reached the top. I backed up against the wall of the top landing, where I couldn't be seen from the hallway outside, to catch my breath. I leaned forward and peeked through the narrow window in the door. I swore I could hear voices.

The hallway outside was clear. I craned my head around to try to see over by the elevator...

There were two Katarovski agents waiting by the elevator. I put my ear to the slight gap between the door and the frame, listening hard.

"...something they saw on the security camera. Probably

nothing, but I thought we should have a look."

"If you say so." I could almost hear the shrug in the second man's voice. "It will not matter. You know the manager will be calling Mr. K."

"All the more reason to be diligent, eh? It can only make us look better."

"From your lips to God's ear, my friend."

I heard the elevator slowly arrive, and the heavy doors open. The voices grew faint, then disappeared.

When the elevator started moving again, I counted a slow ten before I moved to exit the stairwell. I no sooner got the handle pushed and started moving the door than one of the doors in the hallway swung open. I froze.

Petrov Katarovski himself stepped out into the corridor.

Several things ran through my mind right then, but none of them were suitable for print. I ducked back into the stairwell, slamming my back against the wall. My heart raced, thumping in my ears.

There was no conversation to distract Katarovski. He was alone, not even on the phone. He sounded like he might have been muttering to himself.

I hardly dared to breathe. I pushed myself against the wall until my muscles ached, listening intently, staring at the little window, terrified that he would discover me. I needed to make sure this box got into Natalya's hands, and then I needed to get out of there--free. If I was captured now, we could kiss all of our hopes goodbye.

The elevator seemed to move slower than any other elevator I had ever encountered in my life. What if Katarovski lost patience and decided to take the stairs?

Good Lord, there was nowhere to hide in here!

I could hear the elevator, finally approaching the top floor. The carriage stopped, the doors creaked open. Everything seemed to happen in painfully slow motion.

Finally the doors closed and the elevator hummed into action again, beginning its stately descent. Both agents were gone, and Katarovski himself--this seemed like a window of opportunity to me.

I grabbed my cell phone and sent a text to Natalya: I'm here. Then before my nerve could desert me, before any other unexpected person could wander out into the corridor, I pushed through the stairwell door.

It felt like stepping into a different world. I sank to my ankles into the chocolate-colored carpet. The walls sported hip-high glossy cherry wainscoting, and oil-rubbed bronze sconces. It was the sort of the place that made you want to double-check the bottoms of your shoes.

Only two doors opened off of this elegant hall. To my left, a handsome cherry door that matched the wainscoting. A plaque proclaimed this to be the Presidential Suite. And on my right, a glossy white door. Golden gilt formed the now-familiar stylized K, with the ever-present ugly wreath around it. This door had no plaque. I guessed they figured the gaudy family crest was identification enough. It certainly worked for me--I would have recognized the chill that skittered down my spine anywhere.

I raised my hand to knock, but before I could even finish the motion the door flew open. A slender hand closed around my wrist and hauled me through the doorway.

The door clicked shut behind me, sealing me inside the

Katarovski Suite.

♬

I have probably been in gaudier places than the Katarovski Suite, but I would be hard-pressed to name any. What that poor Rolls Royce was to cars, this place was to hotel suites. The walls were glossy, smooth white, and every fixture in the place was a shiny gold color. Glittering, golden K's besmirched every available surface, from the doors of the tall white wardrobes to the white comforters on the beds; from the circular white rug in the sitting room to the big mirror in the bathroom. The bottom of the whirlpool tub bore a K. Even the door handles were great golden K's. The furniture was upholstered in bright gold leather, and every wooden surface had been finished in glossy, opaque white. If you had dared to look up, you would have seen a ghastly K mural on the high ceiling.

It kind of made my eyeballs itch.

"It is not wise to linger in corridors," Natalya said, stepping past me to peer out of the peephole into the hallway. "Everyone is running this way and that--they could be back any minute."

"I noticed," I said. "There did seem to be some brouhaha going on."

"Something about some security camera footage..." She shook her head. "I'm sure it will cause us more trouble in the end, everything does."

I had to agree with that, but it didn't seem helpful to say so. I kept my mouth shut and held out the white box.

"Good heavens! You can't leave that here, Petrov notices everything. That box mustn't be seen!"

I stared at her in confusion. "But--"

She darted back to the door, pressing her face up to the peephole. "Dear God, he's coming!"

"What? I have to get out of here!"

"No time!" Natalya moved like a flash of lightning to the big wardrobe in the living area and threw open the door. "Get inside. Quickly!"

I hesitated, throwing a desperate glance at the exit. "I have to leave, Natalya--I can't be trapped here."

"You'll be seen!" she hissed. "I will get you out of here, but right now you must hide. Hurry!"

If he was in the corridor, she was right. There was no escape. I climbed into the wardrobe and pulled the door shut behind me. I sat down on the wardrobe floor with the box next to me, and leaned back against the side wall, trying not to move, not to make a sound, not to exist. I found that if I held my head just so, I could see through the slight gap between the wardrobe door and the frame.

That was good. It would be nice to have something to watch while I sat in here, for the next God-only-knew-how-many hours, waiting for a chance to escape.

I sure hoped nobody needed anything from this wardrobe.

I couldn't see the door to the suite from where I sat, but I could hear it open and then swing shut again.

"You are back soon," Natalya observed. "What happened?"

Petrov came into the sitting room, glowering like a thundercloud. "You have not been forthright with me, Irena. Why was the Brooks woman sniffing around my car?"

With a sickening, sinking feeling, I realized the security camera footage must have been from the parking garage. I could only hope the angle of the camera had been bad--it sounded like Katarovski had only seen me near the car, not getting out of it.

Natalya shook her head mournfully. "I was afraid she might try something like this. Did she have a white box?"

Katarovski's frown deepened, but he said nothing.

"She tried to give it to me at lunch--she wanted me to deliver it to Alexis. She must still think she can convince me."

"What is in this box?" Petrov Katarovski's voice sounded like giant boulders grinding together.

"How on earth would I know? I refused to accept it. I know my place, and it is not a messenger for Chrispen or Alexis Brooks."

He regarded her thoughtfully. "You know your place. I wonder." Katarovski began to pace across the white monogrammed rug. "You know, I thought it was quite bold of her to come here, knowing the risk to her husband's father. Only now do I realize...Alexei Bruskalov is no longer in any danger at all. Somehow my trap has been sprung, the bait removed. His safety no longer binds them."

"Is this so?" Natalya sounded surprised. "She never spoke a word about it."

"I don't expect that she would, not to one of us." Katarovski paused, considering. "But in light of this, I do not think it would be wise to proceed as I had planned. Alexis Brooks must not stand trial."

"I thought you were eager to see him stand a public trial.

You said that would be the best way to ruin him--out in the open."

"Yes, but not now, you stupid girl!" He threw his hands up and turned his back on her, stomping over to the bar. He uncapped a decanter rather savagely and dumped three fingers's worth of amber alcohol into a glass. "That would have worked beautifully, as long as we could control him. Now--with his father free--there is no telling what he would say. I cannot risk it. The trial must not proceed."

He raised his glass with a shaking hand, and regarded the light filtering through its contents as though he intended to offer it in sacrifice. Standing there with his back turned and his face tipped up, he never saw Natalya move behind him. A metallic flash, a quick motion of her hand, and Petrov Katarovski lay unconscious on the floor, his glass spilling brandy beside him.

I pushed out of the wardrobe, bringing the box from the lab with me. "Sorry for barging in," I said, "but that looked like my cue."

She waved me over. "Hurry! This does not last long." She reached under the bar and dropped a used syringe into the trash.

I whistled appreciatively, opening the box and unwrapping the test kit. "It serves him right to get a shot of that. Those that live by the sword and all that." I handed her the swab. "You had better do this. If I touch him, I think I'll end up killing him."

Natalya knelt by Katarovski's sprawled form and quickly obtained the sample.

"What are you going to tell him when he wakes up?" I

dropped the swab into the plastic vial and sealed it.

Natalya signed the order form with Katarovski's name, with a quick, practiced motion of her wrist. "I don't know. It doesn't really matter--you don't remember anything from immediately before the injection when you wake up, at least I don't. I will blame the brandy. He'll probably lodge a complaint with the hotel."

"Don't let him forget that he decided not to prosecute Alexis."

She shoved the form at me. "Don't worry. I won't. Now get out of here. He will be waking any moment."

I stuffed the order form back into the box with the sample, saluted her, and let myself back out into the corridor. I jammed the box down into the bottom of my purse--you almost couldn't tell I was carrying it.

"Be careful!" Natalya whispered. She reached out and pushed two loaded Makarov pistols into my purse. "Take these with you--one is for you, the other for my father. The guards will be hunting you."

The door to the suite closed with the sharp, heavy click of an automatic lock engaging.

♫

So there I was, in a foreign place, surrounded by unfriendly people, trapped and alone. Oh, and Katarovski agents were hunting me.

What else was new?

I ran for the stairs. The elevator was still out of the question--who knew what waited at the bottom?--but I hurried down the stairs as fast as I could, skipping down the steps so fast my feet barely touched them, my hair bouncing along behind me, hanging onto the handrail like a guidewire, slinging myself around the corner mid-flight to change direction and do it again.

I was almost to the fifth-floor landing when I heard a door bang open below me. A moment later, I heard the one above.

My heart stopped. Several unprintable things skittered through my mind. It had to be the agents--they knew where I was and had closed in on both ends. Thank God I hadn't taken the elevator! The upstairs agent must have just gotten off of it.

I leaned towards the railing, looking carefully down, just in time to see a dark-suited man hop onto the stairs. I could hear the clicking of his hard-soled shoes as he worked his way up.

Holding my breath, I leaned out over the railing and looked up.

A man in mirrored sunglasses with close-cropped dark hair and a suit looked back at me, leaning over the railing above.

I gulped, pulling my head back in, and jumped down the last couple of stairs to the landing.

"She's in here!" The shout rang down from above me, echoing hollowly off the concrete surrounding us. "Between us--move!"

The agent at the bottom started hustling, taking stairs two at a time. The agent at the top pounded down the stairs like a person with no regard for life or limb, barreling through the stairwell as though it wasn't possible to fall down the stairs and kill yourself.

I sprinted for the stairwell door on the fifth floor landing, grabbing it like a lifeline and launching myself through it.

The corridor was thankfully empty, but now what? I had nowhere to go, except--

I leaned on the elevator call button. Cantankerous machinery ground into action somewhere down the elevator shaft.

I could hear the agents pounding the stairs. I looked at the elevator doors, resolutely closed; at the stairwell door-- any moment it would fly open. The thumping footsteps grew louder, closer.

Finally the elevator doors swished open. I dove inside the elevator and punched the lobby button in one desperate motion, then turned fearfully back to face the front.

The stairwell door slammed open.

I leaned on the lobby button, as though holding it in could convey my urgency to the machine.

"She's in the elevator!" The shout rang uncomfortably loud in the quiet hallway, unquestionably the same agent who had shouted from the top of the stairs. The man with no care for his own safety, willing to risk whatever it took to capture me.

I pushed the door close button, over and over, as fast as I could. The big doors finally started moving--slowly, the way this elevator did everything.

The agent stumbled, and for a split second I thought I was free. But no, he caught himself on his hands, recovered, and threw himself at the elevator.

The doors were still closing.

The agent ran for all he was worth. He had lost his

sunglasses when he fell, and I could see his eyes--blue and hard, cold as ice. He flung his hand out toward me, bony and strained, like the hand of Death--

--I screamed--

--and his fingers scratched down the surface of the doors as they sealed shut.

I collapsed onto the floor in a limp, exhausted heap, wiping tears of sheer relief from my face. One agent was on the fifth floor. The other was presumably still running up the stairs. And me, I was in the clear.

My phone chimed--an incoming text message. I had to dig around the lab box to find it. The message was from Natalya:

Trap in lobby, at elevator

For a split second the words seemed meaningless--like my brain just could not accept this new turn of events.

Then I leapt up from the floor and reached for the button panel. The display showed 3, so I hit button 2 with a shaking hand.

"Please stop, please stop," I begged under my breath. If I had hit that button too late, I was completely, totally screwed.

The elevator lurched to a halt. The doors slid open, and I ran out into the hotel's second floor.

I hadn't bought myself much time. The elevator would continue down, they would find it empty, and they would come looking for me.

This corridor was as empty as the others. Lots and lots of doors opened off this hall, doors that could have hidden me, were they not locked. The first door on the right was open, leading to an ice and vending machine room.

But across from that door, on my left, was a door labeled "Housekeeping". I tried the knob, and my heart skipped when it turned in my hand.

The door opened into a small space more like a closet than a room, full of cleaning supplies and implements. Against the wall to my immediate right was piled an assortment of brooms and mops and stick vacuum cleaners. I pushed in among them, leaning back against the wall, and gently closed the door.

It wasn't the world's best hiding spot, but it was the best I had immediate access to. I concentrated on being stone-still and not making a sound. The smell of concentrated cleaning products always made me want to sneeze.

I heard the heavy stairwell door open and close. I listened intently, trying to hear everything that happened in the hallway.

"Second floor, all clear," a male voice announced. I assumed they must be using cell phones to keep each other informed.

The stairwell door opened again, and swung loudly shut.

I counted a slow three before venturing out of the cleaning closet. So one of the agents was working up the stairs. The other was probably in the elevator. If that was true, I had a window while they were busy to escape.

I opened the stairwell door as silently as I could, easing myself in, and checking the stairs above and below me. Everything was clear and quiet, so I hurried down to the first floor.

It was clear down there, too. Hope sprung like a flower

blooming in my chest--I had been right, the agents were busy upstairs, I was really going to escape this place!

The hotel was serving afternoon tea and cookies, and the lobby was bursting with people, alone and in quietly conversing little knots. Threading my way through them was like running an obstacle course.

At last I made it to the grand entrance; I could see the bustling street outside through the heavy glass doors. I felt like singing out loud as I grasped the big brass handle.

A hand clamped like a vise around my upper arm, jerking me away from the exit, spinning me around to face the agent with eyes of ice who had narrowly missed me upstairs.

"Going somewhere, Mrs. Brooks?" he asked, sarcasm dripping from his voice.

I pulled myself up as tall as I could, ready to protest, but before I could form the words a second agent laid hold of my other arm. "Didn't I tell you?" he said. "No need to chase after the rabbit--just watch the hole."

"You are the master," Blue Eyes conceded, and with no further discussion they began propelling me back towards the middle of the lobby.

"If you knew what was good for you," I said, a good deal more boldly than I felt, "you would take your hands off of me."

"If you knew what was good for you," Blue Eyes returned, "you would shut up."

The room fell suddenly silent. As if responding to some signal I could not detect, the crowd of people parted to make a wide path through the center of the lobby.

And who should be ambling toward us from the other

end of that path but Petrov Katarovski, looking none the worse for his artificially-induced fainting spell.

"My dear Mrs. Brooks, why are you here?" Katarovski's tone was warm and friendly, and his arms were spread wide, as though he was greeting an old friend. His manner defused the tension in the room, and the buzz of conversation around us slowly resumed.

The tension in me was not defused. I stood defiant, refusing to buckle under to this man. "I came hoping to convince Irena to deliver a package to my husband." My voice was defiant, too. "You remember him, don't you, Katarovski? The man you have persecuted nearly to death?"

His dark eyes flicked quickly around the room, checking to see if anybody was paying any attention to us. "Search her," he said quietly, coldly, apparently satisfied with what he saw. "Find the package."

But I had his number now. Mr. Big Fancy Politician didn't want a scene, didn't want to smear his already shaky reputation. "Did you bring me here so you could finish the murder you started, Katarovski?" I demanded loudly, argumentatively, drawing the curious stares of everyone in earshot. "Is that why you won't let me go? Are you planning to silence me, the wife of the innocent man you have accused?"

Katarovski's face reddened under the sudden unwanted attention. He held a hand out in front of himself, freezing the agents. "My dear lady," he said, in a voice pitched to carry, oozing with sincerity, "you wound me. I only wished to speak to you for a moment. Your situation saddens me. I have nothing but concern for you." He flicked his hand sharply, and the agents backed away from me. They took up positions that ensured no one would venture too close to Katarovski and I.

Petrov Katarovski took a step closer to me. "This is a dangerous game you are playing, girl," he said, very low. "Do you know why I and all of my men speak English, all of the time?"

I said nothing. I had wondered that myself, but I certainly wasn't going to tell him that.

"America regards me as an enemy," he continued. "When I adopted your language, your silly people lowered their resistance to me. They seem to imagine that since I speak their language, they must share common ground with me. They imagine that they can relate to me, and their fear begins to wane. They are stupid, Americans."

"I am not afraid of you." I refused to let this man cow me.

"You are stupid, too." His voice cut like a lash. "I will not lose this battle to a stupid girl."

I held my chin up high. "I will not lose Alexis to a bastard like you."

Katarovski's face darkened. He released a torrent of impolite Russian words--he looked like he might like to hit something. Katarovski was a man very concerned with how others treated him. "How do you *do* this? I have contested with great men, strong men, with a thousand times your resources and a thousand times your power. And all of them have fallen, every one. How does one miserable, common, stupid girl continue to thwart me?"

"Maybe it's my mule-headed determination. Maybe it's

dumb luck. But do you want to know what I really think it is?"

"Yes!"

I looked at him with utter contempt. "It's because I have something worth fighting for."

I turned and stomped out of the lobby, unmolested by Petrov Katarovski or his agents.

♪

I hired a taxi to take me to the lab. Scott accepted the sample and the order form with its forged signature. I paid him to have the results delivered by courier to my hotel first thing in the morning.

By the time the taxi dropped me off at the Best Western, it was six o'clock in the evening.

I found Alexei pacing the hotel room like a caged tiger. He rounded on me as soon as I opened the door.

"Where have you been? Do you have any idea how worried I was? You might have been abducted--you might have been *dead!* What on earth happened?"

I had never seen him so animated. In his unleashed temper I could see the man who drove the Newton Philharmonic to success all those years ago, the man who walked out in protest when he thought a murderer-gone-free had taken over his beloved orchestra.

I crossed the room and hugged him. "I'm sorry, Alexei. I did not mean for you to worry."

"Well." He patted my back awkwardly, mollified by my extravagant gesture. He looked pleased but relieved when I released him and stepped back. "I am sorry for jumping down your throat, so to speak. But what happened?"

I shook my head. "Honestly, I don't think you would believe me if I told you. Natalya and I ran into a little trouble returning the sample, that's all."

Alexei cocked a skeptical eyebrow at me. "A little trouble?"

I nodded.

"I see. Perhaps we should go have some dinner. You do look as though you've had a rough day. Food might make you feel better."

"Sure," I said. "I don't imagine it can make me much worse."

The evening air was warm and humid. Fortunately we didn't have to walk far at all to find a little cafe with good coffee, homemade pies, and a round booth in the back where we could sit and talk as long as we wanted without being bothered.

I don't even remember what we ate for dinner. I was anxious and distracted, and went through the motions of eating simply from habit.

Neither of us spoke until the remains of dinner had been cleared away, and the waitress brought out strawberry pie and fresh coffee. I think Alexei had been waiting for me to speak first, and I was so far down my own personal rabbit hole I didn't even notice.

"You seem tense," he commented.

It took me a moment to realize that he had spoken. "What's that?"

He laid his fork carefully on the edge of his plate. "I merely observed that you seem rather tense this evening. Is something bothering you?"

"Everything's bothering me."

"That...doesn't really help."

I laughed, a short, barking laugh with no real humor in it. "I suppose you're right." I sighed. The strawberry pie looked perfect and smelled delicious, but all of the sudden I had no desire at all to eat it. "Katarovski's government puppets are dropping the case against Alexis."

His eyebrows shot up. "There will be no trial? But this is wonderful news!"

I shook my head. "I hate to deflate your hopes, but I don't think it's necessarily good at all. Katarovski is dropping it because he doesn't want Alexis to testify to what really happened, not because he is giving up. He'll make another move. I just wish I could figure out what it will be."

Alexei picked up his fork and attacked his pie with renewed vigor. "Many have wished for a window into the mind of Petrov Katarovski," he said. "It is enough for me that my son will go free."

"But that's just it. Through all of this, Katarovski has never intended that Alexis should go free. Since Natalya first came to Zwickau, that has never changed. I don't believe that he intends for a second to just let Alexis go."

My cell phone chirped in my purse. I flipped it open--I had a new text message from Natalya.

Alexis released tomorrow 9am

There was an address after the message. I had to read the whole thing twice to make sure I wasn't just reading into it what I wanted to hear.

"They're releasing Alexis in the morning?" I blurted in surprise.

Alexei whistled appreciatively. "Katarovski's government friends must be highly placed indeed to get things done so quickly."

"Indeed." My mind was racing. "They are announcing this rather late--if they actually even announced it at all. Katarovski must be hoping to avoid too much media attention. And Natalya obviously thinks we need to be there--Alexei, I would bet you anything Katarovski doesn't plan to let Alexis walk away tomorrow."

"But where on earth would they take him, with so many people watching?"

"That's just it. He isn't expecting much of anybody to be watching at all. And even if some media do show up, all he has to do is leave. After the fuss is over and everyone leaves, his agents can grab Alexis and follow. Katarovski has experience disappearing people in Russia."

Alexei looked stricken. "You are right. This is a ploy to get Alexis out of the public eye, to relocate him to where he can be handled. Where are you going?"

I stood up and gave the waitress a "rounded up" handful of cash to cover our meals. "Dankeschön," I told her, and turned back to my father-in-law. "Back to the room. I need a phone book and an internet connection. We have some calls to make."

He scrambled out of the booth to follow me. "Wait! Chrispen, I don't understand."

"Katarovski wants this release done with as little attention as possible, right?" I grinned, but it felt predatory, skin stretched across teeth in a grim slit. "We are going to make sure he gets some attention."

"Attention?"

The slit widened. It felt like my face might actually tear. "We're going to give him a media circus."

♫

The night was black as coal; the sky hung heavy with clouds and not a single star shone through. The moon was a vague patch of faint glowing light.

It was well after midnight when the two figures, silent and as dark in their matching suits as the night outside, moved into our hotel room.

If the devil himself had flowed in as smoke through the keyhole, he couldn't have been any quieter, or intended any greater evil.

Nothing stirred in the dark room, so they moved further inside. The sloppy, formless lump under the blankets on the bed closest to the door seemed unaware of their presence, and slept on.

The men raised matching pistols, each equipped with a silencer, and fired several rounds into the motionless form on the bed.

Their grim mission accomplished, the men lowered their weapons. One of them stepped closer to the bed, grabbed hold of the blankets, and yanked them off, revealing a bullet-riddled...lump of pillows?

Before either man could really understand what he was seeing, I popped up to kneel where I had been lying on the floor between the far bed and the wall, my borrowed Makarov trained on my would-be assassins.

"I told you Katarovski wouldn't be able to resist snuffing me," I said, "now that he knows I'm here. Are you getting this?"

The closet door behind the two startled men was open just a crack. At my words, it opened entirely, and Alexei stepped out. In one hand he held a camcorder, specially geared-up for night filming. In the other he handled the second Makarov with a casual competence that surprised me. I had practiced many hours, and completed my concealed carry certification. Where did Alexei come by his familiarity with firearms?

"I am," Alexei answered. "Drop your weapons, please, gentlemen."

One of them muttered a Russian curse, but they both complied.

"So you are the one who stole those weapons," the agent farthest from me said. I could hear hatred dripping from his words. "We were harshly punished for their loss. I should have known we would have you to thank. It seems you are the root of all of our problems."

Alexei flipped on a light, and I realized with a cold start that I knew this man. It was the same blue-eyed agent who had pursued me with such inhuman ferocity at Katarovski's hotel.

Alexei retrieved the discarded pistols from the floor and moved them out of reach. I grabbed the top sheet from the bed closest to me, twisted it into a long coil of homemade rope, and tied the first agent's hands behind his back. The icy, baleful stare on me never wavered--I wondered if I should have restrained Blue Eyes first.

"The root of your problems," I told him, pulling the sheet from the other bed and twisting it as well, "is that really awful man you work for. I am doing nothing but attempting to save my husband. The day you moved against Alexis was the day your problems began, and you have no one but Katarovski to thank for that."

"You will regret this," he hissed.

"The only thing I regret is not plugging both of you the minute you walked into this room. But I guess that would make me no better than you." I stretched my jury-rigged rope in my hands and stepped behind him, reaching for his arm.

Quicker than thought, he spun to face me, and his fist crashed into my face. I stumbled backward and landed on the floor, disoriented and dizzy, seeing stars.

The agent piled on, straddling me with both hands locked around my throat in a crushing grip that made breathing impossible. He wasn't looking at me, though. He glared daggers at Alexei.

"Drop that gun and untie my partner," he growled, "or the woman dies."

Alexei regarded us over the barrel of one of pistols the agents had dropped, complete with silencer. "I fear you misunderstand your position." Alexei's voice was rock-steady. I clawed at the agent's hands, but for all the effect it had I might have been buffing his fingernails. "If you do not release her, I shall fire."

Blue Eyes dug his fingers into the skin of my neck. "You are a coward and a traitor, Alexei Bruskalov. You haven't the stones to shoot a man, even to save this worthless female. Now drop it or she dies!"

Alexei fired a single shot. The agent flew backwards off

of me, leaving burning scratches on the sides of my neck.

Alexei came to me and helped me to stand. "Are you all right, *dorogaya?*"

I nodded, holding a hand against my throat, and swallowing hard. It hurt.

The agent lay on the floor, writhing and arching his back in pain. His shoulder was bloody and slick. He made no sound, though, not a whimper or a cry.

I jerked him up to a sitting position, grabbed the twisted bedsheet and lashed his arms together behind his back.

He sucked air between his teeth in a pained hiss. "You have made your last mistake. Petrov Katarovski will grind you to dust beneath his heel!"

I folded my arms. "You keep getting it wrong." I gestured at the camcorder in Alexei's hand. "Do you see that? Do you realize that camera is the property of CNN? Do you realize that they recorded a long interview with us yesterday evening?"

The agent looked from the camera to me. "You are lying. There is no way they would have believed you."

"Think what you like. They believed enough to leave us equipped to capture any move you made. This footage, combined with that interview, will be most compelling when they broadcast it."

"You are dreaming. The world will never see any of that. Petrov Katarovski will not allow it!"

"I think we've gone past the point of worrying about what Katarovski will allow." I sighed. "You can stop recording, Alexei--they wanted footage of the attack, and they've got that." I turned back to Blue Eyes. "Did you know that camera is uploading that recording as we speak? There is no suppressing this. Tell me, what is he planning to do with Alexis?"

"You are wasting your time. He will never tell you that." The other agent surprised me when he spoke. He had a gravelly voice, and sounded altogether too wise to be involved in a mess like this. He shook his head. "Nor will I."

"Well, then," Alexei said matter-of-factly, "your words are of no further use to us, are they?" He gagged them both with towels from the hotel bathroom.

There was not much to do at that point but wait for the courier from the lab. The tell-all interviews we had given the night before and the video footage CNN was receiving even now would ensure a strong media presence at Alexis's release. Whatever was going to happen, would happen in front of the world.

Alexei ran out and brought us back breakfast, and we passed the slow hours in a tense, uneasy silence.

It was a few minutes past six when the courier knocked on the door. I opened the door just enough to accept the manilla folder he offered, tipped him, and went back into the room.

Of course the results confirmed what we already knew to be true. All of the pieces were in place. The only thing left to do was face Petrov Katarovski in the final battle for my husband's fate, a battle he had personally assured me he did not intend to lose.

We hung the Do Not Disturb sign on the door, and walked out into the crisp morning air.

Petrov Katarovski's face turned a mottled purple when he saw the mass of people gathered for the official release of Alexis Brooks. Flashbulbs popped, cameras rolled, journalists scribbled in steno pads, and newscasters monologued into microphones. It was precisely the sort of chaos he did not want. Natalya stood behind him, wearing something suspiciously similar to a smirk.

Alexei and I had been there for the last hour, giving statements and interviews. Mr. Katarovski would, we believed, find this particular media audience a bit less cordial than usual.

He recovered his composure quickly, holding his hands up for quiet. "My friends! My dear friends, how wonderful to see you all here today."

"Mr. Katarovski, can you tell the press why you are here today?" The question came from an earnest young man in the back who had been especially sympathetic to our story. Alexis Brooks fan? Katarovski conspiracy theorist? Perhaps. I hoped he was both--I was glad to see the questions starting and hoped the group would continue to press him.

Irritation flickered across Katarovski's face, smoothed away almost before it fully registered. A wide, warm smile replaced it. "I must warn you that I cannot tarry long for questions. We are on rather a tight schedule, and I do hope to have my daughter safely away before the man is released. God willing, she will never suffer his presence again."

I snorted in unkind amusement. A nearby journalist quirked an eyebrow in my direction, and I faked a coughing fit, waving her off. I could not malign Katarovski's sincerity, after all; doubtless he hoped fervently that Natalya and

Alexis would never be in the same room--or indeed the same country--ever again.

Of course, if Alexis was conveniently murdered, Mr. K would not have to worry.

"I am here this day," Katarovski continued, picking up steam, finding his rhythm, his voice ringing across us, the assembled throng, "to bid a final farewell to this sad, sad man before returning to the homeland he and his father have both tried on very different levels to destroy."

"That's a lie," I said conversationally.

The journalist glance my way again, then turned back. "Mr. Katarovski," she called, each word clear and precise, "I spoke yesterday with Alexis Brooks. The story he tells is very different, and quite compelling, involving days of harassment and torture at the hands of your hired bodyguards."

Katarovski was already shaking his head, mournfully, as though someone's regrettable personal failures had been dragged into view.

"It is the truth!" Natalya leaned as far past him as she could, shrieking. "Alexis is telling you the truth! I was not kidnapped--I was only trying to escape *him!*" The look she gave Katarovski was withering. "This man has--"

Without warning, her eyes rolled back and she crumpled into an unmoving heap at his feet.

"I do apologize." Katarovski's tone was sober. "I cannot imagine what that monster has done to her, but she is still prone to fainting when she speaks of it." He shook his head. He seemed genuinely sad, a believably distraught parent-- except that he made no move to help her. He regarded her there, unmoving on the ground like a doll tossed carelessly aside, and turned back to the crowd. "His story is a lie, nothing more--a diabolically clever excuse that he somehow brainwashed my daughter into parroting." He waved a hand. "All of this 'harassment' and 'torture' is nothing more than the paranoid ranting of a completely self-centered mind--a man who really does believe the entire world revolves around him."

He smiled graciously for the popping flashbulbs and the rolling cameras, and gestured to one of his guards as Natalya began to stir. The guard bent and helped her to her feet, seeming quite solicitous but keeping an iron grip around her upper arm.

"My dear, dear friends, it has been a pleasure speaking with you as always, but it is time for us to go." The closer Katarovski got to his ultimate escape, the thicker he laid it on--his voice practically glistened with an oily film of sincerity; so much warmth weighted it down it seemed a wonder his words reached us at all.

"Before the tearful parting, I wonder if I might say a few words." My voice wore nothing but sarcasm and carried clearly. And yet to judge by the reaction I received, I might not have spoken at all. I pushed myself off the concrete ledge where I had perched next to Alexei thus far and cut through to the front of the crowd--one way or another I was going to make them listen. I had to. Katarovski was not going to deliver his carefully-chosen soundbites and then ride away into the sunrise. It wasn't going down like that.

"You!" Katarovski spun to face me. His skin looked pasty, like uncooked dough. Like someone who had seen a ghost. From his perspective, maybe he had.

"None other." I inclined my head.

"How can you dare to show your face here? Have you no shame?" The accusing finger he pointed in my direction shook, with anger or fear.

These questions seemed pretty rich, coming from him. "I've nothing to hide here, Katarovski." I had meant for my tone to be mild, but it carried the sting of accusation. "Can you say the same? I am here only to see that the truth gets told." Although, I had to admit, no one seemed to be falling over themselves to listen to me. I might be worth a quick interview when no one better was around, but when a newsreel headliner like Petrov Katarovski entered the room, I turned pretty near invisible.

Katarovski pulled himself up to his full height, his face closing like a fist, turning dark and blotchy. "There is nothing you could say that anyone here would care to listen to, Chrispen Brooks! The facts of this case have been established. Why would any person with their wits about them pay any attention whatsoever to a woman crazy enough, stupid enough, to marry a known murderer? If it's attention you seek, you won't find it here, woman!"

I stood blinking in the heat of that blistering diatribe. There were so many things in his little speech that made me want to repudiate them immediately, I couldn't decide where to start. Katarovski glowed with obscene confidence, aware that he had won.

"Do you have any comment, Mrs. Brooks?"

I jumped. The voice belonged to that same young reporter who had interviewed Alexei and me earlier. I turned to face him, and found the crowd waiting silently, microphones extended, cameras rolling. Katarovski had denounced me so thoroughly every person there held their breath to see how I would respond.

"My only comment," I said slowly, "is to repeat what I told Mr. Katarovski earlier--I am here to bring out the truth." I glanced over at the agents--I did not wish to 'faint.' "That woman is not Irena Katarovski. Her name is Natalya Bruskalov, and the Katarovski's kidnapped her thirty years ago. The story of Alexei Bruskalov as a traitor was a cover created specifically to remove the family so that they could get to her. Irena Katarovski died when she was three years old, and Natalya has been forced to live her life in her place ever since."

The place was instantly abuzz. People shouted questions, people pronounced me crazy, people offered the opinion that if this was the best I could come up with to excuse Alexis, the situation must be pretty damned desperate.

Petrov Katarovski stood still as stone, pale and grim and unmoving as the furor raged around us. He stared at me, and I regarded him, chin held high, until quiet was gradually restored.

"Mr. Katarovski," called another voice. "Do you have a response to this allegation?"

"I think," he said, turning from me to the crowd with a grand, sweeping gesture, "that the word *allegation* gives undue credit to this ridiculous notion. I pity this woman, and her evil husband--think of the mental gymnastics they have performed to concoct the tale you have just heard. How terrible it must be to twist one's mind that way--almost as terrible as the crimes which drove them to it."

He could talk, there was no question about it. He cast a practiced eye over his audience, assessing their response to him. What he saw must not have entirely pleased him, because he stepped forward and continued to press his case. "This story, it is crazy, is it not? Almost as crazy as we would have to be to accept it strictly on the word of one desperate woman who is obviously a good deal less than sane herself." He ran a hand through his unkempt hair, giving every appearance of a man pushed to the very limits of his reason. "The scheme she has proposed is no small thing. Falsifying a case of treason, spiriting a child away from one family, and planting her in another--such a thing could not be done in secret! Where are the accomplices? Where are the witnesses? If such a terrible thing truly occurred, where are the people who saw it happen?"

"Here is one," Alexei shouted. "I am Natalya Bruskalov's father."

Katarovski shook his head sadly. "I might have expected something of this nature. Your daughter's disappearance is well known, Bruskalov--but does the loss of your child excuse the taking of someone else's?" He spread his big hands wide open, the picture of earnest sincerity. "My friends, this man cannot be trusted. His interest here is clear and vested--he would believe any young woman to be his daughter, to ease his own pain. This whole story is ridiculous--this is why she can produce no objective witnesses. Now we really must--"

"Actually, I believe I qualify as an objective witness." The voice rumbled like thunder from the back of the crowd, carrying effortlessly over Katarovski's rant. As we watched, the mass of people parted to make a clear path for--

"Dmitri Kast!" I gasped. The world seemed to waver in front of me. "I am so glad to see you--I was afraid you were dead!"

He smiled his gentle, craggy smile. "Evidently I am not." His smile faded and his face hardened as he turned to Petrov Katarovski. "I can vouch for the truth of everything Mrs. Brooks has said, and I would be happy to share my full story with any of these fine members of the press."

Katarovski's eyes bulged dangerously. "This...is...hearsay!" he finally spluttered. "Any number of people may conspire to say a thing is true, that does not make it so! My friends, how long are we expected to entertain this nonsense?"

I snorted. "I couldn't agree more. We've been sidetracked with your silly demands for witnesses, Katarovski." I turned to face the crowd, holding up the manilla envelope from the lab. "I have here results from DNA paternity testing for the lady we know as Irena Katarovski, against both Petrov Katarovski and Alexei Bruskalov. Would anyone care to guess what the results conclude?"

Nobody made a sound, not even--to my surprise--Petrov Katarovski. The moment was as still and fragile as glass. It felt like the entire world leaning in, holding its breath. Finally I dared to dart a glance over my shoulder.

Petrov Katarovski was the picture of living, breathing, seething fury. He was so livid he actually shook where he stood. His face was dark and swollen, and the veins in his temples throbbed ominously. If you didn't know any better, you might have thought he was choking. I doubted anyone had ever seen him this irate--and lived.

I braced myself for the verbal onslaught, the protests and accusations that I knew would be coming. Of course no lab test is one-hundred percent accurate--even DNA-based paternity tests are occasionally wrong. The chance of both tests giving inaccurate results was vanishingly small, but it was the only chance he had and I expected him to jump on it.

What I did not expect was the great big semi-automatic pistol he pulled out of his coat and leveled at me. Before I could blink, the agents had their weapons drawn as well, aimed out in an attempt to cover the crowd. Someone screamed.

Katarovski grabbed Natalya savagely by the arm. "This woman is the future of the motherland," he growled, "the direct heir of the sainted Joseph Stalin. She is destined to carry on his noble work and mine. Destined! No one shall interfere with this divine duty, do you hear me? No one!"

His eyes burned, they glowed from within with the unholy light of city skylines aflame in the night, of torches bobbing through the evening in the hands of the unruly mob. It was the peculiar light of insanity, and if you have seen it once you will never mistake it again.

He turned and dragged Natalya to the waiting Rolls Royce, preaching ferociously to his own imagined choir about mother Russia and father Stalin and the sacred virtue of returning to one's roots. The agents covered his quick retreat, then hopped in the front seats and fired up the car.

"He's got that poor girl!" Apparently our screamer also had a tendency to state the obvious. "Somebody stop him!"

I reached into my purse and hauled out the silenced Makarov, running out into the street, taking as careful aim as I could manage under the circumstances.

Snick, snick--two silenced shots in quick successions.

"It's just another day at the firing range," I muttered to myself.

--snick, snick--

"--just another few targets down at the range--"

--snick, snick--

"--just a group of targets that happen to be spinning, and moving away from you, and in uncomfortably close proximity to people." I lowered the pistol and wiped the sweat from my forehead.

Six shots fired, four tires blown out, no casualties. I wouldn't win any marksmanship prizes, but I had stopped the Katarovski-mobile. It screeched and swerved to an undignified halt, sideways in the street like a toy car tossed aside by a giant child.

The back door flew open and Katarovski came charging out, brandishing his weapon and cursing so quickly it was impossible to pick out individual words.

"You just cannot stop interfering, can you, woman? You could have left well enough alone and lived, but no--you keep making yourself a thorn in my side! No more, do you hear me? No more!"

He raised that big gun.

I was numb with fear, I couldn't feel my hands or my feet--but I understood what I had to do. I pulled the Makarov up and lined the sights up with that hateful, horrible man, squeezed the trigger--

--and heard the hollow click of an empty cartridge. I was out, and I was dead.

Katarovski laughed a shrill, twittering laugh, the unhinged sound of a madman.

"Noooooo!" The shout--the desperate, wailing shriek came from somewhere behind me, and before I had placed it, Alexis threw himself in front of me, panting, arms thrown wide. "Do what you want to me, Katarovski, but I won't let you touch her!"

Alexis. The world seemed to stand still for a split second while my brain reeled. I hadn't even been aware they released him. It seemed like forever since I had seen him--I certainly had not imagined our reunion like *this!*

"How noble!" Sarcasm dripped like acid rain from Katarovski's voice. "How gallant! How *stupid!* Don't imagine, boy, that I have any problem disposing of the great Alexis Brooks!"

I grabbed Alexis's arm. I thought I had maxed out my capability for fear, but that was before Alexis was at risk as well. There was no time to run, nowhere to hide; Katarovski was already sighting down the barrel of that monster of a pistol.

A shot ripped through the street, rending the very air. I flinched, clutched at Alexis, trying to figure out where he was hurt--

--and Petrov Katarovski crumpled in slow motion, down to a motionless heap on the road. It was probably the most graceful thing he had ever done, oddly out of place with the wet crimson stain quickly covering his shirt.

What? I couldn't seem to keep up at all--any way I looked

at the situation I could not figure out how Alexis and I were still standing.

Natalya crawled out of the Rolls Royce, carrying an agent's Makarov pistol.

Katarovski rolled his eyes around to look at her. "Irena, how--why..."

She looked down at him. "My name is Natalya. You stole my life. I have only repaid the favor."

The silence held a moment longer, and then noise seemed to burst from everywhere at once--reporters frantically narrating events, questions shouted by so many people in so many different directions it was impossible to follow them all, police officers attempting to restore some order to the situation. My skin felt cold and clammy; I was light-headed and numb as it began to sink in that I would not die here after all.

Alexis turned around face me. "My God, Chrispen, are you okay?"

I tried to answer him but the words just wouldn't come. I was alive and he was alive and those simple facts filled me with a profound happiness that the carnage around us could not touch. I had never seen a more welcome sight than Alexis, now clean-shaven and back in his street clothes. He had never looked more handsome, and the gratitude I felt just to have him in my life overwhelmed me. Everything I had been through, everything we all had risked, was as nothing next to this great flood of emotion. And I was completely unable to put any of it into words.

"Chrispen?"

I stepped closer to him, and my lips found his. His arms

went tightly around me, and the clamor around us melted away. An entire world narrowed down to him, and me, and the warmth we shared, the rising need for one another that a year together had not begun to slake.

A long moment later I rested my head on his shoulder, at peace for the first time in a week.

"I love you, too," Alexis whispered in my ear, and I knew he had heard everything I had not said.

FINALE

The release and the momentous events that accompanied it happened on the morning of June eighth--our first wedding anniversary. Our gift that year was simple and priceless--our continued lives together.

June eighth was also Robert Schumann's birthday, and the date of the concert with the Philharmoniker Zwickauer.

Of course, with all the intervening insanity, you would think the concert would have been a definite no-go. I know I did. Zwickau and everything that had happened there seemed like another lifetime.

But the crowd in that Berlin street had barely dispersed before Alexis's cell phone rang; the conductor of the Philharmoniker had been following the television coverage of our saga closely. The anniversary concert was still very much on, he said, and Alexis was still very much invited to play.

To be honest, I thought he was half crazy for asking. And I secretly wondered if Alexis wasn't more than half crazy for saying yes. Everything that had happened that morning had consequences--the first of which was all of us spending that morning giving detailed depositions for police reports. With so many witnesses and so much documentation, there was not really any question about which crimes had been committed and whodunnit, but everything had to be handled properly.

We were still in Berlin when we learned of Anya Katarovski's apparent suicide. The Katarovski Estate had burned to the ground. Her wedding ring and her mother's ring were found in the charred remains of her bedroom, the room where the fire started--where the fire was deliberately set.

"She called me on the telephone," said Agent Blue Eyes on the news report, as distraught as it was possible for a man with a heart of ice to be. "She told me of the anguish she suffered at her husband's murder, of the kerosene she was using to prepare herself and her room for the flames, even as we spoke. I tried to reason with her, but...I could not stop her."

I was stunned. I mean, I had known she wasn't playing with a full deck, but still--I had not expected this. The Katarovski's had both seemed too strong, too determined, to fall victim to such despair. The constant television coverage of every aspect of our situation and Natalya's made me nauseous, and very ready to be done and out of there.

But still, with all of that, we somehow managed to make the drive back to Zwickau in time for the concert. It wasn't quite like coming home--more like coming back to a childhood haunt when life has put a few miles on you. You have changed, and the fact that the place is the same just emphasizes the difference in yourself.

The Hotel Sachsen Zwickau was like a living embodiment of that principle--everything looked just as it did the day we had left. The manager had evidently been following the news as well, and comped our stay for the night, in the same suite where the whole crazy adventure had started.

Wilhelm Braun personally delivered our violins to our suite. "I am so glad to see you well," he told me, pumping my hand in an enthusiastic handshake, gripping my upper arm with his other hand, "so very glad. I hope that if there is anything I can do for you, you will not hesitate to ask."

We barely had time to pause in the spacious rooms, could spare no more than a regretful glance for the king-sized bed beckoning from the bedroom. A quick shower to make us human again, and we had to hurry into town to find Alexis something he could wear at the concert. After that we hurried to the concert hall, so Alexis could get in a little practice and warming-up before the performance.

"I don't know if I can do this," he said, standing in an ill-fitting off-the-rack tuxedo, regarding his violin doubtfully where it rested in its case. "This is crazy. I should never have agreed to this."

"You worry too much." I moved behind him, and rubbed his shoulders. "You're going to do just fine, you'll see. You could play this concerto in your sleep."

He turned suddenly to face me, catching my hands in his, his eyes awash with anguish. "Yes, but--"

"Shh," I cut him off. He was right; this went far beyond the reach of empty platitudes about how much he had practiced. "I know. You have every right to be concerned. You haven't eaten or slept properly in days; you haven't even seen your violin in days. You don't really have your strength back yet from what those men did to you. It's too much to ask for you to perform a demanding concerto.

"But you will. You'll get up there and you'll do it for the same reason that you said yes when they called you."

"I had a reason?" he said dryly. "I can't see it from here."

"This is what you came here to do," I said simply. "If Katarovski takes that from you, even though he's dead, he wins. I know you won't let that happen. But even beyond that, the world has been following your story this past week. And after this morning they know everything you've been through, everything you've suffered. They know how hard this will be for you. And when they come to the theater tonight, or tune in to watch your performance on television, they are going to be inspired by what you do. And seeing you stick through this is going to give them the courage to stick through whatever is going on in their own lives right now."

He leaned over and kissed the top of my head. "Thank you."

"You're welcome, of course. Now I'd better get out front. You're going to knock them dead."

Was it the most brilliant performance Alexis had ever

given? Well, no--after everything he had been through? Of course not. But it was a fantastic performance all the same-- the strain of it was evident in his pale face and the uncharacteristic quiver in his arms, but he played with a fire I had not heard before.

How many violinists could have pulled that off? I couldn't think of any--the simple fact that he performed at all seemed like a kind of miracle, a superhuman feat every person in the audience appreciated fervently.

I stood in the cheering, applauding crowd in Ballhaus Neue Welt, with Natalya on my left and Alexei on my right, clapping my hands with tears in my eyes. The glittering, bejeweled crowd around me seemed to *get* it; they really seemed to understand how important this performance had been to Alexis, how he'd had to fight for it, and that made it, in turn, equally important to them. We had been to hell and back since signing on for this concert. Our lives would never be the same.

But in the end, we found more through the Lost Concerto than had been taken away. Tomorrow, we would begin our journey back to the States, go free my mother from my uncle's place, and put her life right again. And right here, right now, healing for wounds thirty years old, and for those more recent, could finally start. Families could be rediscovered, bonds rebuilt, those who had lived as strangers for decades could know each other once again. Husband and wife, father and daughter: all were reunited.

And that, I thought, was worth fighting for.

Meet the author online at

www.sandra-miller.com

Find out more about the Alexis Brooks series at

www.alexis-brooks.com